FLYAWAY VACATION SWEEPSTAKES!

This month's destination:

Exciting ORLANDO, FLORIDA!

Are you the lucky person who will win a free trip to Orlando? Imagine how much fun it would be to visit Walt Disney World**, Universal Studios**, Cape Canaveral and the other sights and attractions in this area! The Next page contains tow Official Entry Coupons, as does each of the other books you received this shipment. Complete and return *all* the entry coupons—the more times you enter, the better your chances of winning!

Then keep your fingers crossed, because you'll find out by October 15, 1995 if you're the winner! If you are, here's what you'll get:

- Round-trip airfare for two to Orlando!
- 4 days/3 nights at a first-class resort hotel!
- $500.00 pocket money for meals and sightseeing!

Remember: The more times you enter, the better your chances of winning!*

*NO PURCHASE OR OBLIGATION TO CONTINUE BEING A SUBSCRIBER NECESSARY TO ENTER. SEE BACK PAGE FOR ALTERNATIVE MEANS OF ENTRY AND RULES.

**THE PROPRIETORS OF THE TRADEMARKS ARE NOT ASSOCIATED WITH THIS PROMOTION.

VOR KAL

FLYAWAY VACATION
SWEEPSTAKES

OFFICIAL ENTRY COUPON

This entry must be received by: SEPTEMBER 30, 1995
This month's winner will be notified by: OCTOBER 15, 1995
Trip must be taken between: NOVEMBER 30, 1995-NOVEMBER 30, 1996

YES, I want to win the vacation for two to Orlando, Florida. I understand the prize includes round-trip airfare, first-class hotel and $500.00 spending money. Please let me know if I'm the winner!

Name_____

Address _____ Apt. _____

City   State/Prov.   Zip/Postal Code

Account #_____

Return entry with invoice in reply envelope.

© 1995 HARLEQUIN ENTERPRISES LTD.   COR KAL

"I believe you've forgotten something."

Katie frowned, and carefully examined herself in the full-length mirror. "Like what?"

Dakota took a small velvet box out of his pocket.

"All brides should wear her rings, especially newlyweds," he said as he took her unresisting left hand and gently slid two rings on her finger.

Katie fingered the sparkling engagement ring and its matching wedding band. "You were awfully sure of yourself, weren't you?"

"Truce?" He covered her fingers with his. Her hand was soft and warm and feminine. "It would be a good idea to wear the rings—they come with the territory."

"I suppose I have to." She took a deep breath. "But don't think for a moment that I'm going to—"

"Hush," Dakota said softly. *So it was going to be hands off, was it? Not if he had anything to say about it.*

"One more thing, Katie. If I remember correctly, this goes with the territory, as well." He lifted her face to his and before she could utter a protest, he captured her lips in a searing kiss.

Dear Reader,

"Whether you want him for business...or pleasure, for one month or one night, we have the husband you've been looking for. When circumstances dictate the need for the appearance of a man in your life, call 1-800-HUSBAND for an uncomplicated solution. Call now...."

We're so glad you decided to call the matchmaking Harrington Agency, along with the second of the five desperate singles who'll be looking for their perfect stand-in mate in the new "1-800-HUSBAND" miniseries.

You're in for a fun-filled frolic as you join Mollie Molay's Katie O'Connor, who certainly has her hands full with not one—but *two!*—handsome "husbands"!

Look for all the 1-800-HUSBAND titles, one per month from now through December.

Regards,

Debra Matteucci
Senior Editor & Editorial Coordinator
Harlequin Books
300 East 42nd Street
New York, New York 10017

Mollie Molay

HER TWO HUSBANDS

Harlequin Books

TORONTO • NEW YORK • LONDON
AMSTERDAM • PARIS • SYDNEY • HAMBURG
STOCKHOLM • ATHENS • TOKYO • MILAN
MADRID • WARSAW • BUDAPEST • AUCKLAND

My thanks to the proprietors of The Tickle Pink Inn,
Carmel, California, for their gracious permission to use
the inn as the background of my novel.

To Julia, Deborah, John and Michael for their
sense of humor, love and support.
I'm proud of you all, too!

ISBN 0-373-16597-8

HER TWO HUSBANDS

Copyright © 1995 by Mollie Molé.

Chapter One

"Do you have a spouse, Katie?"

Neil Gibson, chief executive director of Toyland Industries steepled his hands, propped his chin on two well-manicured forefingers and regarded Katie O'Connor, his new marketing assistant.

"No, sir."

"A significant other?"

"No." Katie felt herself redden. Gibson was more than twice her age, and even if significant others were fairly common nowadays, it was hardly a subject she felt comfortable discussing with him. "No, I haven't. Why do you ask?"

He seemed not to hear her. Instead, he read aloud from a pastel pink-and-blue promotional brochure she'd handed him.

""The Tickle Pink Inn at Carmel, California, thirty-five rooms, including eight suites, most with private balconies and fireplaces in all rooms. Spa tubs, daily continental breakfast, evening wine and cheese, lush terry-cloth robes, fresh coffee service in all rooms. Honeymooners our specialty.""

He lifted his gaze from the brochure and smiled at her across his giant-size mahogany desk. "Quite impressive. I take it you're proposing we hold this year's business conference in a honeymoon hotel?"

Prepared to defend her choice of meeting sites, Katie leaned forward in her chair. "Actually, sir, the Tickle Pink Inn is a small honeymoon *inn,* but it does have a fully equipped conference room that will accommodate ten people."

"A secret business conference in an inn that caters to honeymooners? A bit unusual, wouldn't you say?"

"That's exactly the point, sir." Katie straightened up with pride. "I know this meeting is extremely secret. No one would think to look for a business conference in this type of location."

Gibson paused to appreciate the point. "You're certainly right about that, Katie. I have to commend your ingenuity in coming up with the idea. However..." His voice faded as he continued to turn the pages of the brochure.

Katie glanced around the spacious office. Decorated in shades of burgundy and forest green, burnished brass lamps topped with black shades on the large mahogany desk, and deep leather chairs, the room resembled a private study instead of a corporate office.

Shelves of toys successfully developed and marketed by the company lined the walls. Dolls, board games and action figures vied with computerized toys for space. The karate figure that had set the pace for last year's toy market occupied a place of honor. It was only one of the toys that had made millions of dollars for Toyland, a company she'd come to admire after spending countless dollars buying its products for her small niece and nephew.

"We've had some problems with security lately," Gibson finally said. "Maybe this is the answer. Naturally, I'll want you to attend as the conference coordinator, and to see to it our presence there doesn't leak out." He glanced back at the brochures. "Of course, if you were to go by yourself it might cause questions. We can't have that, can we?"

"We can't?" was all Katie could manage. The hairs on the back of her neck started to tingle when she connected his earlier question about her romantic status with the calculating look that came across his face. She sensed something was about to happen when he pressed a button on his intercom.

A deep voice answered. "Smith, here."

"Come on in my office for a few minutes, Dak. I have someone in here I'd like you to meet."

Katie's sixth sense went into overdrive. Gibson was about to play some kind of trick on her; she knew it. Maybe it was the gleeful look on his face, because she couldn't think of a thing she'd said to make the man appear so pleased with himself. When there was a light knock on the door, she braced herself for trouble.

The door opened and a tall man with sun-drenched brown hair and an unconscious air of self-assurance that enveloped him like a cloak entered the office. "You wanted me, sir?"

"Yes, come in and sit down."

Katie silently inhaled. The person who'd answered Gibson's summons was the man she'd seen many times around the building. A man who'd captured her interest from the first time she'd laid eyes on him and even then had sensed his animal magnetism. He nodded politely as he moved past her and dropped with lazy grace onto a high-backed chair adjacent to hers.

The burgundy leather upholstery formed a perfect background for his tousled hair and tanned features. She couldn't help but stare.

"Dak, I'd like you to meet Katie O'Connor. Katie is fairly new to our marketing division. I've put her in charge of ramroding this year's new product planning conference. Katie, meet Dakota Smith, the head of our security division."

"Dakota?" she said, coughing to hide the sudden catch in her voice.

"Just call me 'Dak,'" he replied amiably, as if her reaction was an everyday occurrence. "The name is a joke my parents played on me when I was born, a sort of tribute to where we lived at the time. I guess they figured with a name like Smith I needed an unforgettable first name. 'Dak' will do just fine."

She cleared her throat. "I'm sorry. It's just that the name is very unusual." And so was the rest of him, she thought as she took in his hazel eyes, the riveting cleft in his chin. Rugged features, broad shoulders and at least six feet three inches of lithe masculinity were definitely not attributes of the usual type she'd seen walking around Toyland since she'd been here—or any other place, for that matter.

For a few moments, his amused gaze locked with hers, then his eyes roamed over her in a way that made her shift in her chair. She'd been eyed in that manner before and had managed to ignore it, but this time it was the patronizing smile on his face that annoyed her.

"Katie's doing a great job arranging this year's conference. You'll be interested to know she's booked it into a honeymoon hotel."

"Actually," Katie interjected as she saw a frown come over Dakota Smith's face and his eyes widen in surprise, "it's an inn."

"A secret business conference in an inn that caters to honeymooners?" He snorted his disbelief and shook his head. "Perhaps you didn't know picking the site for the annual toy selection conference was my job?"

He glanced at Gibson, who raised his eyebrows and shrugged. The fact that Gibson was going along with her seemed to add to his annoyance.

"You can't be serious!"

He stared hard at Katie, as if expecting her to agree.

"It's a perfect location for a meeting that's supposed to be highly secret," she replied in as calm a voice as she could muster, aware she must sound slightly defensive, and angry because of it. She fought to keep her voice businesslike. "The point is, no one will suspect a business meeting is going on."

"She's right, Dak," Gibson broke in as he tossed a brochure at Dak and thoughtfully turned the pages of his own copy. "Nothing wrong with attempting something new. We've tried everything else to stay ahead of those foreign toy pirates, and still secrets keep leaking out. Remember the cruise we took several years ago? I wouldn't have thought a soul knew what we were planning, but the news was out by the time the boat hit dry land."

"Come on, Neil," Dak cut in, "it hasn't been as bad as all that. I run a damn good security department, and you know it."

"Maybe so, but I can't take a chance. This year's lead toy is not going to turn up duplicated in the Orient, if I can help it. Nor are copies going to show up at the New York toy fair next February."

"Well, perhaps it might work," Dak said, ignoring Katie's presence and speaking directly to Gibson. "But can Miss O'Connor guarantee this meeting will be held in the highest secrecy?"

"Yes, Dak, I can," Katie retorted. She was annoyed at being referred to in the third person, as if she weren't present, and her voice carried a distinct note of anger in spite of herself. When Dak's cold gaze locked with hers, she shot him a black look. "And furthermore, in order to ensure secrecy, in my proposal I've suggested the spouses of the five attendees come along. Since the specialty of the inn is honeymooners, their absence would draw notice."

Dak shrugged and tossed his brochure on Gibson's desk. "Have it your way, then. Just make certain everyone appears to be on some kind of honeymoon."

"Glad you feel that way." Gibson nodded complacently. "Because I brought you in to tell you that I expect you to attend the conference, along with Katie."

Dak's gaze swung from his boss to Katie. She felt a ripple of apprehension when a faint smile curved at his lips and he eyed her with interest.

"Sure. No problem."

Who did this Dakota Smith think he was! Katie fumed silently as she fussed with the papers in her hand. He might feel he was God's gift to women, but he certainly wasn't hers.

"By the way, there *is* a slight problem." Gibson leaned back in his chair and chuckled as Dak's attention swung back to him.

"Problem?" Dak's eyes narrowed at he gazed at Gibson. "How's that?"

Katie tore her irate glance away from Dakota Smith and fastened it on Gibson. Whatever joke the man had in mind, she had the uneasy feeling that she wasn't going to like it.

"I propose that the two of you go up to the Tickle Pink Inn as man and wife to allay suspicions. A marriage of convenience for a few days, you might say."

"That's a horse of another color. Count me out," Dak snorted, then surged out of his chair and strode to the picture window that overlooked Santa Monica's pristine beach. Sunlight streamed through the windows, highlighting the angry glitter in his eyes and outlining his rigid stance. He raked his fingers through his hair as he gazed out at the sun-kissed ocean, then back to Gibson. He took a deep breath. "As far as I'm concerned, there's no marriage that's convenient. Marriage is a pain in the neck and in the bank account. One was enough for me."

"You can count me out, too." Stung by Dak's attitude and comments, Katie gathered her materials and prepared to leave. "I wouldn't go as this man's wife if you paid me to do it."

"That's just the point, Ms. O'Connor. I *am* paying you to plan the conference and all that it entails. That includes going as Dak's wife."

Gibson's quiet voice flowed over her like a stream of ice-cold water. Gone was the genial teddy bear of a man who surrounded himself with toys. His friendly smile had disappeared, replaced by a cool, challenging stare. An upraised eyebrow told her he was waiting for an affirmative answer, that he wouldn't settle for less. Annoyed as she was by Dak's attitude, she

saw clearly she was going to have to swallow her reluctance to have him accompany her to the conference. She really had no choice, especially since Gibson
liked the idea of the Tickle Pink Inn and had praised
her plans.

Tight moments passed as both men studied her,
Gibson with an implacable gaze, Smith with resent-
ment bordering on anger. Finally, she reminded herself she was a professional woman in a man's world
and this was just another assignment, after all. A week
as a "bride" might not be too high a price to pay for
the job she'd been working toward for four years. And
not when Toyland's next year's sales were possibly
riding on the successful outcome of a brainstorming
session at the Tickle Pink Inn.

"Just what would this 'convenient marriage' en-
tail?" she asked, not completely convinced she was
ready to be a bride. She returned Dakota Smith's angry gaze with a cool one of her own.

"Now, Katie, calm down. I'm not suggesting anything more than an appearance of a marriage. Just in
case someone might wonder why two single people
were staying at a honeymoon inn."

"Hell, married or not married, people go away together all the time and no one thinks anything about
it." Dak broke away from the window and turned to
Gibson. "All the time," he repeated. "So what makes
the difference in this case?"

"Only if they stay in the same room, Dak."

"In the same room?" Katie rose to her feet and
clenched her hands. This was going too far. "Surely
you're joking, Mr. Gibson!"

Gibson shrugged and allowed himself a brief smile.
"Not at all. Let's face it. You'd be bound to draw at-

tention if you booked into separate rooms at a honeymoon inn. You'd be the subject of interest and gossip and before you knew it the secret would be out. Especially since it would become evident you work for the same company. However, if sharing a room bothers you, book a suite."

"Anyone care to ask me if I want to go along with this fool idea?"

Dak's frustration showed in his clenched fists and in the way he glared at her, as his hazel eyes bored into the green of Katie's.

She returned his scowl with a frown of her own. As long as he felt the way he did, she was going to put an end to his insulting ways...immediately. "The truth is, Mr. Gibson—I'm already married. We've kept it a secret for, ah, personal reasons. But I see now that it's best to let you know under the circumstances."

"Don't understand why it has to be kept a secret, Katie, but have it your way. In any case, it's no problem. Just bring your husband along." He glanced over at Dak. "Now that that's settled, we'll have to do something about you."

Dak snorted and turned back to study the ocean. Hell, he thought, there was something about this Katie character that was too pat to be true. A faint warning thought stirred as he mulled it over. She was sharp, all right, but so was he. He'd watch her like a hawk, "married" to her or not.

"No, thanks, I can take care of myself."

"See that you do, and don't take it out on Katie. She's doing a fine job with this assignment," Gibson announced. He leaned forward in his chair, motioned to the shelves of toys that lined the office. "The reason behind Toyland's success is that as a company it's willing to try something different, something innovative. That includes strict secrecy, so that cheap counterfeits don't flood the market and steal our thunder. The novel idea of a conference in a honeymoon inn falls right in line with those policies, young man, even if it wasn't your idea." He fixed Dak with a long, silent stare, and seemed to ignore the mixed emotions showing on Katie's face. "Besides," he continued, "our stock has begun to slide. We may be facing layoffs, or worse. I refuse to let Toyland be counted out. Now that Katie understands the facts and is willing to go along with me, how about you?"

Dak ran his fingers across his chin, closed his eyes for a long moment as if in prayer. "I'm not sure what it is that you want me to do, now that Miss O'Connor here is already married."

His bland features and calculating glance as he turned to gaze at her told Katie that he had something on his mind. So did she.

"Find yourself a wife. I want you to be at the conference."

"A wife! Any chance that you'll change your mind about this ridiculous idea, sir?" After studying Gibson, Dak finally made a last appeal. "I'm sure I can think of something more acceptable."

"Not a chance." The firm look Gibson returned was unmistakable. "I like Katie's idea. There's a lot at stake here."

"I still think holding a conference at a honeymoon inn is a spacey idea. But if you're so dead set on holding it at the Tickle Pink Inn, I guess I can live with it." Disgust radiated from him like a dark cloud.

Katie bridled and started to leave. "I'm not sure I can!"

Gibson rose from his chair and threw out a hand to stay her. "Hold up, Katie. I'm sure Dak doesn't mean anything derogatory. Give it a try, Dak. Things might work out better than you think." When Dak reluctantly nodded, Gibson handed Katie back the fanciful inn brochures. "Dak, take Katie somewhere private for coffee and let her explain her game plan. Outside of the two of you, I want you to see to it that only the conference attendees are informed of where we're going and why. And—" he rose for emphasis and came around his desk "—not a word of the true nature of the stay to their spouses. Just let each of them be told it's a bonus second honeymoon from the company, or whatever you like. And be sure to remind our people their jobs are at stake if anything leaks out on this one. Not only that, we've a proposal or two coming down the pike that's also strictly hush-hush.

"And you, Katie, I expect you to ride herd on those people, keep them from asking questions. When meetings are in session, tell the spouses their other halves are out golfing, or fishing, or anything else that's plausible. And do anything to keep them too busy to wonder where our team disappears to."

Katie noted the change in Gibson. Now that things were settled to his satisfaction, his benevolent look had returned. He appeared complacent and very pleased with himself. Too bad she didn't feel the same way. But it wasn't the time to argue with him, even if she'd wanted to. Certainly not after he'd praised her plans for the conference and when her job was at stake. If anyone had done her in, it was herself with her suggestion that the conference be held in a honeymoon inn. She nodded, murmured her reply and gathered her brochures and her portfolio. She had to find a husband, *fast*. She halted in her tracks as she heard Gibson softly add behind her, "And, Katie, you will try to get along with Dak, won't you?"

Casting a long, silent glance of reproach at Gibson, she hurried out of the office, followed by Dak. She sensed his disapproving presence as he followed her.

No sooner had the door closed behind them than Katie confronted him. "I hope you realize I'm no more fond of attending a conference with you than you are with me, Mr. Smith, husband or not."

"You'll have to do better than that at the inn, Katie O'Connor, or everyone will wonder what's going on. After all, we work for the same company. We should at least be friendly." A wry look spread over his face as his gaze swept her from head to toe.

"Nothing is going to go on between us," she hissed, "and don't you forget it. I'm a married woman and my husband will be coming along."

"Still, we'll have to work together, won't we?" His raised eyebrows challenged her.

She brushed him away. "Don't get smart, and quit patronizing me. Teaming up with you wasn't my idea. In fact, you'd be the last man I'd want to have as a partner, let alone a husband, legally or otherwise."

"Is that so?"

Dak studied her in a way that made her check the buttons on her blouse.

"What have you got against me? We hardly know each other."

"That's true," she agreed, "and I'd like to keep it that way. Now, I'm pretty busy at the moment. I haven't time for coffee, or any more of your remarks. If you want to talk, call my secretary for an appointment this afternoon. I'll fill you in with what you need to know then—that is, if you think you have the ability to keep an open mind."

You'll do more than that, Katie O'Connor, when I'm through with you, Dak thought as he watched her disappear into an office down the hall. *Husband or no husband, you're going to find out who's in charge here.*

Hell, she hadn't even batted an eye when she'd been told selecting a conference site should have been his job. After his one attempt at marriage, he'd had it with aggressive women. As for Katie, he'd have to watch his back in order to protect his own job. In this partnership, it was going to be one where he'd be the boss. And if she wanted to fight, well then, he'd oblige her.

"STELLA, GET ME the personnel folder of a Katie O'Connor. She works in marketing," Dak called to his secretary as he entered his office. Without waiting for an answer, he strode into his inner office and opened the door to a small refrigerator built into a bookcase. Bottles of Evian water, diet colas and juices were lined in neat rows. Too bad there wasn't any hard liquor in there, he thought as he uncapped an Evian. After what he'd just been through, he sure could have used something stronger right about now. Hell, he thought as he dropped into his chair and took a deep swallow, he'd finally managed to get rid of one woman, and here he was about to be involved with another female just like her. The irony of it all was they were so much alike they could have been twins.

He threw his head back against his chair. Talking about marriage brought back memories he'd had a devil of a time putting behind him and would just as soon have forgotten. His divorce had been two long years in the making, and he hadn't been single long enough to feel like a bachelor again. Damn.

He'd spent a year making his ex realize there wasn't a thing she had to offer that he was still interested in, and another year inching his way through their divorce. In the process, he'd given up most of their bank account—not that he cared a hoot about the money— and a lot of his pride.

Good thing they hadn't gotten around to building a nest, or having children, or loving after they'd stopped being in love.

"The O'Connor file, Dak."

Stella's voice telegraphed her disapproval as she took a tissue out of her pocket, picked up the empty Evian bottle to dab at the wet rings it had left behind and laid the slender personnel file on his desk.

"What's Katie been doing that's made you interested in her?"

"Katie? You know her?

"Sure do—we're friends. She's a sweet person, isn't she?"

"I hope she turns out to be," Dak muttered. "I couldn't stand it if she wasn't."

"Are we talking about the Katie O'Connor who works over in marketing?" Stella was incredulous. "What's she done to get you so upset?"

"She hasn't done anything—yet." He frowned as he turned pages of Katie's personnel file. "But look here, Stella, be a good kid and forget I mentioned her. It's just that I was so deep in thought I ignored my own rules about talking too much."

"Talking too much? You never do, especially about women. I'm around you for at least eight hours a day, five days a week, and you've never even mentioned any of the women around here before, let alone Katie. In fact, you seem to have made it a point never to involve yourself with anyone who works at Toyland. Now you're talking about being angry at Katie O'Connor and you expect me not to discuss it? She's a friend of mine. How can you expect me not to talk about her?"

She bit her lip when Dak raised his head from the file and fixed her with a warning glare. "Okay, okay, but something strange is going on."

"You couldn't be more right. Now, close the door behind you and forget you ever brought me O'Connor's file."

"I left an out card with your name on it in personnel files. When you're through, be sure to give the file back to me to replace."

"Go back and remove the card. For now, I don't want anyone to know I have the file."

"If you say so, but you're sure acting out of character. Chief of security, huh!" Stella sniffed her displeasure and backed out of the office.

Out of character. It was a good thing Stella didn't know how much different he was about to get. He thought of Gibson's instructions. Get himself a wife? Not while he had a breath left in his body! The whole damn caper was ridiculous, and the more he thought about it the more he distrusted it. Caution was practically his middle name; he wasn't the head of security for nothing. Yet here he was, about to do something at Gibson's whim, something his instinct told him was going to be nothing but trouble. Especially since he had to work with a woman like Katie O'Connor.

Of course, under other circumstances, knowing her might have been interesting. With her petite figure and tasteful clothing, she was an eye-catcher, to say the least. She obviously had a brain, or she wouldn't have gotten the job in marketing. Pretty, too, if you liked redheads. He had, at one time. Too bad he and Katie were off to such a poor start. He put thoughts of her charms out of his mind and studied her personnel file.

More than curious about the woman who was going to be his partner for a week, he scanned the pertinent information pages. Katie O'Connor was twenty-six, single, with auburn hair and green eyes. Height and weight: five feet four inches, one hundred and fifteen pounds. No attachments, lived alone in a leased condo in the Valley. Relatives: five brothers, one married with two small children, three unattached and one a broker at a well-known securities firm. No arrests, not even a traffic ticket.

She'd graduated from UCLA with a major in marketing and a minor in journalism. Grade-point average: 3.4. Belonged to all the right organizations, including the most sought-after sorority. Worked her way through college as a dancer. Interesting, he thought. How unlike the strictly businesslike image she tried to project. He made a mental note to check the reference.

Upon graduation, she'd interned at Kaiser Toy Distributors and had accepted a job there in marketing. Worked at Kaiser for four years, rising through the ranks from intern to the administrative assistant to the director of public relations. His eyes paused at her work experience—Kaiser Toy wasn't exactly a rival of

Toyland's, merely a distributor instead of a manufacturer, but he stored the information in the back of his mind for further study and moved on.

No previous marriages or divorces. His gaze swung back to what he'd just read. No marriages? She'd told Gibson she was married. And why would she keep her marriage a secret for personal reasons? His mind went into overtime and a smile covered his face.

Except for that telltale red hair and the secrets hidden in her personnel file, Katie O'Connor was too good to be true.

Chapter Two

He lounged against the Tickle Pink Inn's registration desk as if he were waiting for her arrival. Hands in the pockets of his charcoal gray business suit jacket, and with a disapproving look that left nothing to her imagination, he straightened and glanced at his watch. "Well, Miss O'Connor. You're late."

Katie felt a shock wave go through her. She'd experienced the same sensation when he'd stridden confidently into Neil Gibson's office: an inner response to Dak's unconscious self-assurance and male sensuality. On the other hand, she thought sourly, it was unlikely he wasn't aware by now of how he affected the women who had the misfortune to cross his path.

His gray suit complemented his cinnamon-colored hair. Against a pristine white shirt, a paisley tie duplicated the color of his hazel eyes. He looked innately strong and masculine, and as if he'd just walked off the cover of *GQ*. Whoever had guided his choice of clothing obviously had a deep understanding of the aura of sensuality that clung to him, she thought darkly. And, to her way of thinking, he made the most of it.

The only detail out of place was the Mickey Mouse watch he wore on his wrist.

"I don't know what you're talking about," she finally managed, hoping he didn't realize how attracted she was to his appearance and to the man inside. "I wasn't aware I was supposed to meet you here."

"Come on, Miss O'Connor. Loosen up. You're not afraid of me, are you?"

"I'm afraid of a lot of things," she replied ambiguously, raking him with questions in her eyes.

"Like what?" Dak countered with a raised eyebrow and a lazy smile.

"Please, let's not waste time talking nonsense," she said, deciding he probably used that very smile to snare his targets. "What are you doing here?" To hide her reaction to his mind-boggling question and to him, Katie pretended to look for something in her purse.

"Since when is doing my job a waste of time?" he remarked as he straightened and strolled toward her. "Checking on the security of the conference site *is* what I'm supposed to do, isn't it? Of course," he went on, sarcasm dripping with every syllable he uttered, "unless you think that security is your job, too?"

Katie dropped her purse and, frozen in place, watched her compact, lipstick, car keys and a small notebook slide across the floor. "I don't know what you're talking about," she gasped as she made a lunge for her rolling tube of lipstick.

"If you're trying to tell me you didn't know selecting a conference site was my job, forget it. As far as I can see, Miss O'Connor, ambition is your middle name. Maybe you have something to prove, but I haven't. But as long as we're stuck with this caper, I'm resigned to working together." He held out his hand. "Truce?"

He wanted a truce after he'd just gotten through insulting her again? If it wasn't for Neil Gibson's parting words admonishing her to get along with Dak and her knowing how much of Toyland's future rode on the success of the conference, she would have told him what she thought of him and his offer. Instead, she stuffed her belongings back into her purse. "I'm not sure this partnership is going to work, Mr. Smith."

"Call me 'Dak,' since we're going to be partners. And we are. Don't you ever doubt it. And, with your *permission,* I'll call you 'Katie.'"

He didn't wait for her answer, but seemed to take it for granted that she would go along with him.

"I know how to do my job. You just do yours." He glanced behind her. "Where's your husband?"

Katie's heart plunged southward. She wasn't used to lying. Somehow she was afraid the truth was written on her face for him to see. "Working, of course. However, he'll be along for the conference."

"Working," Dak echoed as he studied her. "Of course. Well, let's get to work. The manager, Mrs. Fraser, left to get the keys to the boardroom where the conference will be held. She'll be back in a minute. You can inventory the amenities while I check out the security of the room and the surrounding area."

He was too agreeable. Katie's sixth sense quivered uneasily.

Mrs. Fraser, a large motherly type, chatted amiably as she led the way down the gray-carpeted hall and into the small, well-equipped Terrace boardroom. Decorated in the inn's trademark colors of gray and pink, it was a miniversion of Toyland's own impressive boardroom. A cherry-wood conference table surrounded by ten chairs occupied its center. Computers, telephones and audiovisual equipment stood at the ready. In one corner there was a table with neatly stacked paper pads, pencils, water pitchers and glasses.

"Of course," Mrs. Fraser explained to Dak, "we'll be glad to furnish anything you find missing. As for meals, if you intend to serve them in here, you'll be able to choose from a variety of menus. But we do hope you all will join us in our dining room."

To Katie's annoyance, she continued as if Dak were only present.

"We try to make your stay here as comfortable as possible, without detracting from your main purpose." She smiled coyly. "This is, after all, a honeymoon inn. A place where one is supposed to get acquainted or reacquainted with one's spouse. Of course, we understand the need to conduct business. Still, the honeymoons should come first, don't you agree?"

"You bet, Mrs. Fraser. And we won't let our people forget it, will we, Katie?"

She nodded coolly. It was the first time he'd given an indication that he was aware of her presence, or had included her in the conversation. As for Mrs. Fraser, she could see questions forming in the woman's eyes. Before they could be asked, Katie spoke.

"Now, about the software program you use in the computers...?"

"It really doesn't matter," Dak interjected. "We'll be bringing our own computers, and taking them with us when we leave. And we'll bring our own cellular telephones and copier, as well."

"Goodness, it all sounds so mysterious." Mrs. Fraser worried her bottom lip; a frown creased her forehead. "But, of course you may do as you wish."

Deeply chagrined, Katie recognized Dak was right. Of course they would bring their own equipment. There would be nothing left to chance. No one could tap their telephone conversations, or retrieve information buried in the computer hard drive. She gazed at him with grudging respect. He might be an unlikable chauvinist, but at least he knew his job.

"Well, I'll leave you two to talk things over." Mrs. Fraser turned to leave and touched Dak's arm in passing. "You do know where to find me, don't you, Dak?"

Katie glowered as he smiled his reply. She might have known he'd make it a point to get to the inn before she had and cultivate Mrs. Fraser. He'd wasted no time in using his charm on the woman.

"How about some lunch, Katie, or do you need to look around some more?"

Lunch with that womanizer? No way. Let him use his charms on Mrs. Fraser. She took a quick, last look around. "I don't have time for lunch, thank you," she said, "but I would like to take a peek at the room accommodations before I leave."

"Don't tell me you actually booked the place sight unseen?"

"Not at all." She was annoyed to find herself on the defensive, a decidedly uncomfortable position. "After I studied the brochures, I spoke to Elly Fraser on the phone. And furthermore, the inn was recommended by a friend of mine who spent her honeymoon here. All I really needed to verify was the conference facilities."

"Katie O'Connor, you're lucky I'm in this with you." Dak shook his head and eyed her with disapproval. "You'd make a poor security operative if you're ready to sign up on someone else's say so."

"It was never my intention to be in the security business," she shot back. "In spite of what you think, I'm very happy to leave the sleuthing to you."

"Temper, temper, Katie." He shrugged. "Of course, what else can I expect from a redhead?"

She bit back a retort. As a lifelong redhead, this wasn't the first time she'd been accused of having a temper. Her five brothers had teased her unmercifully about the color of her hair. But she wasn't going to give him the satisfaction of getting a rise out of her. She glanced at her watch. "I've got to get started. At the rate I'm going I won't get home until late tonight."

"I'm sure your *husband* will understand if you're late getting back. By the way, what did you say his name was?"

Katie's mind came up empty. For the life of her, she couldn't remember if she'd mentioned her husband's name when she'd impulsively blurted out that she was married. "Ken," she said, improvising.

"Ken. Any last name?"

"Why are you so interested in my husband anyway?"

"No particular reason. Just being friendly is all."

Dak wasn't going to tell her he knew the truth about her single status and a few other secrets. Not yet. Not when there was the slightest chance she'd gotten married since signing on with Toyland. But there was a guarded look in her eyes that told him she was trying to hide something. And not doing too well.

When people married in California, a community-property state, they had to have their records changed to reflect their new marital status, he knew. For insurance and tax purposes, if for nothing else. Katie should have known that, too. But in the five months since she'd been hired, she hadn't had her records changed. It was his job to find out why not . . . and if she was really married.

It still rankled that not only had she chosen the conference site without consulting him and had taken it "upstairs," but she'd turned him down as her husband, when she clearly needed one. "So, how about it. Lunch before you leave?"

"No, thanks." She took a pen and small notebook from her purse. "I have to make a few notes on what we'll need before I go. And I still want to look at a room or two."

"Well then, see you back home. I'll check in with you tomorrow and we'll go over your notes."

He lingered in the doorway while Katie scribbled a few remarks in her notebook. To his surprise, the more she got her dander up, the more she appealed to him. Maybe it was her body language when she was cornered that got to him, the way her eyes sparkled when she was angry or her quick wit when she deflected questions about her nonexistent husband. She'd caught his interest, to say the least. But, no matter how true that was, the feisty redhead sure acted guilty as hell.

CLASPING THE KEY to a suite, and with Mrs. Fraser on her heels, Katie opened the door to the pink-and-gray grandeur of room 105. A luxurious eight-foot couch, piled high with fluffy pillows and fronted with a brass-

and-gold coffee table, stood against a wall made of solid windows. A twenty-five-inch television set, complete with a black box for cable and a VCR, covered another wall. A serving cart held soft drinks and bottled water, a silver ice bucket and a basket of munchies. A coffee service occupied a corner of a bar.

Her feet sank into the deep pile of the carpeting as she opened the sliding doors to the suite's bedroom. A canopied king-size bed, cherry-wood nightstands and an enormous armoire filled the room. An open door led to a bathroom with a sunken tub that resembled a scene from the *Arabian Nights*. Katie was excited to think that in a short time she'd be occupying a suite just like this one for the week of the conference.

"The accommodations will do nicely if they're all like this." She handed the keys back to Mrs. Fraser. "In fact, I've never seen anything so beautiful."

The lady beamed at the compliment. "Thank you, my dear. We try to please. As long as you like it so much, I'll make certain it's the one you and your husband will occupy when you come next week. He liked it, too."

"He did?" Katie stopped in her tracks. Her husband liked it, too?

"Oh yes, Mrs. Smith. Dak not only admired it, he told me he was certain you would want it for yourselves."

"You must be mistaken," Katie answered, her mind on ways to murder Dak. "I'm not Mrs. Smith."

"Of course not. Not yet," Mrs. Fraser apologized. "I put the cart before the horse, didn't I? It's just that Mr. Smith told me you were getting married next weekend."

Katie froze. "He did what?"

"Oh dear. I've said too much, haven't I?" Mrs. Fraser apologized again as she patted Katie's hand. "I won't tell a soul. Not that it will matter after next week. By the time you come back to the inn you will have been married, won't you? Until then, don't give it another thought. No one up here knows about you but me, do they?"

"No, no one knows me. Especially Mr. Smith." Katie said emphatically as Mrs. Fraser's eyes widened. But he was going to find out a thing or two about her before another day passed. Especially that she didn't enjoy being taken for granted. She handed the woman the keys and left.

Her next move was clear. From the enigmatic look on Dak's face when he'd asked her husband's name, she knew he had something up his sleeve. She needed to get home and find a husband, fast.

On the long drive back to Los Angeles, she mentally reviewed her options. Maybe she'd ask one of her brothers to do her a favor and pose as her husband. No, they didn't need another reason to tease her. She certainly didn't have a male friend she wanted to have around that closely. On the other hand, maybe she'd be better off finding a stranger.

The last time she'd listened to one of her favorite talk programs on the car radio, the syndicated program Dr. Love, she'd heard a telephone number for the Harrington Agency. 1-800-Husband. It was the perfect solution to her problem.

"I'm happy to see that you had guts enough to show up today," Katie announced when Dak sought her out the following morning. "What in heaven's name did you have in mind when you told Mrs. Fraser that we were getting married next week? Especially after I told you I was already married!"

"So you did." Dak moved toward a chair in front of her desk. "Mind if I sit?"

"And if I objected, would that stop you?" She wasn't really surprised when he shrugged and plopped into the chair.

"No, not really. Do I have to remind you we have a job to do?"

He didn't have to remind her. Not with Neil Gibson's threat to initiate layoffs still echoing in her mind. Maybe even her own job was at stake. As far as she could see, her future at Toyland depended on the success of the conference.

Katie took a deep breath and started again. "Now, look here, there's no need for an attitude. I don't like Gibson's orders any more than you do. My guess is that you're smarting because he said there have been security leaks around here." She felt a moment of satisfaction when she saw his eyes flash before he caught himself and gave her a lazy smile that didn't quite reach his eyes.

"Neil is overly paranoid about secrecy. As a matter of fact, there haven't been any major leaks about our products on my watch, and that's been several years."

"That's not the impression I received," Katie said, eyeing the studied smile on his face. His chair was close, too near for comfort. Especially when the faint scent of his cologne teased her senses. "Gibson said there was a major problem a few years ago."

"There was. That's why I have the job now. So, do you want to talk about the conference, or shall I tell Neil you've decided not to participate?" He leaned forward to pick up a paperweight off her desk and juggled it in his hands, while his eyes dared her to say no.

There was a soft knock and the office door opened. "Katie?" Nancy Wiggins, Katie's secretary, walked gingerly into the office, cleared her throat and gazed wide-eyed at the sight of her boss and Dak Smith. "Oh, I'm sorry, I didn't know Mr. Smith was in here with you. I didn't mean to interrupt something."

"You're not interrupting anything, Nancy. Mr. Smith and I were just talking."

"Why don't you tell Nancy the whole truth? I'll bet she's heard all about it already." Dak rose to his feet, strode around the desk, pulled Katie up after him and planted a kiss on her lips.

"What are you—" Dak's large hand at the corner of her mouth pretending to caress Katie's lips prevented her from finishing her sentence.

Nancy colored. "Yes, sir. I have."

"Have what?" Katie demanded.

"Come on, Katie. Don't be coy. Nancy only wishes us well, don't you, Nancy?" He wrapped his arms around Katie and smiled over her head at the flustered secretary. In an undertone, he whispered in Katie's ear, "Go along with me. I'll explain later."

Out of the corner of her eye, Katie could see Nancy gape as Dak's lips brushed Katie's ear.

"Get your hands off me," she muttered. When he held her more closely, Katie called to her secretary, "Don't believe a word this man says, do you hear?"

"Katie, I know you're hung up on keeping our relationship a secret, but..." His eyes telegraphed a silent warning at her. "What will people think if they see us honeymooning without first hearing we intended to get married?"

Her heart sank. Did he know the truth about her being single? Was that why he was acting this way? At any rate, the whole office staff would be aware of her supposed engagement to Dak by lunchtime, and the entire building, too, before five o'clock. She groaned into his shoulder as Nancy murmured another apology and left.

He smelled faintly of spice and other exotic scents, of soap and sexy cologne. The scent stirred her senses as it wafted her way. It wasn't fair. He was too damn attractive. The way her luck was going, she'd have a hard time keeping him from finding out the truth, considering what he was doing to her.

"You know she'll tell everyone she sees about this, don't you, Mr. Chief-of-Security?" Katie mustered what little dignity she had left and shrugged out of Dak's arms. "For a man whose job is to keep a tight lip, you're mighty free with words."

"Only when necessary. Only when necessary." The satisfaction in his voice gave him away.

"You deliberately started the rumor we're going to get married, didn't you?"

"Maybe."

As far as she was concerned, there was no maybe about it. "How could you? What will my husband think if he hears about this?"

"I don't know, Katie. He gazed at her under raised eyebrows. "What *will* he think?"

Looking at him, Katie forgot she'd intended to call the 1-800-Husband number, to visit the Harrington Agency in San Francisco and hire herself a husband for the conference. She was too engrossed in the lingering warmth of Dak's arms around her, his breath whispering past her ear, his cool lips on her own. Even of the scent of his cologne assaulting her senses when he'd held her closely to him. Too closely. Sensuous thoughts she seldom allowed herself to entertain swept over her, raising goose bumps, yet at the same time suffusing her with heat and guilt.

She considered him through narrowed eyes while he strode to his chair and sank his solid strength into its upholstery. What was this man doing to her, or worse yet, why was she letting herself respond to him this way?

Chiding herself at her reactions to his pure animal appeal, she waited until he'd made himself comfortable. He was only another man sent by fate to annoy her, she reminded herself. She'd handled his kind before and she'd do it again before things went too far.

"Now, listen here," she said to him briskly. "I told you I'm married. I don't know why you're persisting in this foolishness. You're only making a fool out of yourself, and me, too. Let's get this straight. You've mauled me for the first and last time. It's hands off from now on, understand?"

His ex-wife had spoken to him in just the same manner the night she'd slammed out of the house. The same night he'd given up on his marriage and left for good.

He'd had more than enough of his ex, and of Katie, too. He might not have been the perfect husband, but he was a spouse no longer. Katie O'Connor needed to learn she wasn't going to order him around. But first, he had to have her cooperation, even if it killed him. Damn Neil Gibson and his bright ideas!

"Oh, and how do you propose to appear like a newly wedded woman at the inn if you expect me to keep my distance?"

"I'll have my husband with me, that's how!"

"You surprise me, Katie. If you show up with a husband, you'll shock me even more."

"Then brace yourself for the fireworks of your life."

"Go ahead. Pull out your big guns, Katie. I'm ready."

He eyed the blush that turned her creamy complexion a bright pink. Interesting, he mused, pink *does* go with red. And the deepest emerald green eyes he had ever encountered *could* turn even greener. From that moment on, he forgot she reminded him of someone else. Katie O'Connor suddenly became a desirable woman, and the prospect of perhaps sharing a pseudo honeymoon with her more than a little intriguing. While he didn't look forward to the hard time her expression promised, he was red-blooded enough to see beyond it to future possibilities.

He caught himself in midthought. Pretty sure that nothing was going to change her determined character or his, either, he still had to find out if she was married. If not, he was determined to be the happy groom, no matter what she wanted. Anyway, the way it looked it was going to wind up being part of his assignment when she showed up without a husband, wasn't it?

He gazed thoughtfully across the desk at Katie. "Of course, it *would* be better if we got to know each other more before we reached the inn."

"I don't understand what you're driving at." Katie gazed at him, caution written in her eyes and in her taut body language.

"Right now, we're more like strangers than lovers...."

"Hold it right there! We *are* strangers!"

"Not for long, Katie O'Connor, not for long. Unless you turn up with a husband, we're going to be more than strangers whether you like it or not." Dak unfolded his length from the chair and winked at her. "See you later."

As he left the office, he glanced over at Katie's secretary. With an expressive shrug of his broad shoulders, he said into her wide eyes, "Lovers' quarrel."

"Katie?" Nancy came to the door as soon as Dak waved goodbye. "Are you really going to marry him?"

To Katie's disgust, envy was written all over her secretary's face as she gazed longingly after Dak and back to Katie.

"Maybe." Katie hated to lie, but the fact was she hadn't gotten around to going up to San Francisco to choose her hired husband, and Dak was acting mighty strange. If she ignored Gibson's warning about appearing at the conference without a husband, she'd be in big trouble. She'd have to take a day off and fly up to 'Frisco to get the job done. The sooner the better.

"How come I didn't even know about it?"

"Maybe because I didn't know about it, either," Katie muttered as she straightened her papers.

"You mean he proposed to you right out of the blue?"

"You can say that." She tried to keep out of her voice her annoyance at Dak's high-handed manner and the way he traded on his attraction for every woman he encountered. Trust the man to gather women the way bees gathered honey!

"How romantic! I wouldn't have guessed such a thing was going on. You sure know how to keep a secret.'' Nancy clasped her hands to her chest and sighed. "And about Dak Smith!"

"What's so special about him?"

"How can you ask a question like that? You're going to marry him. If anyone ought to know, it should be you!"

"You're a romantic, Nancy. There's more than one reason to get married, you know."

"Love is the only reason I know. Gosh, Katie, you're so lucky. All the women in the building will die with envy."

"Great! Now, if you don't mind..."

Nancy shot her another envious look and dashed out the door.

Katie gave up the pretense of working and sat back in her chair. She touched her lips and thought about Dak. Of the strength in his arms and the kiss he'd given her. His lips had been soft and warm when he'd brushed hers with his own. She'd even felt a faint regret when the kiss was over. It might have been a game to impress Nancy, she knew that, but she wondered what the kiss would be like if they ever really connected.

KATIE COULD HEAR the voices of the secretarial pool as the women left for lunch. She closed her office door and settled down to double-check the plans for the meeting at the Tickle Pink Inn. Sunlight splashed through the windows and across her desk. Reluctant to close the shutters and hide the inviting view of the blue Pacific and the waving fronds of the palm trees that lined the oceanfront boulevard, she finally shoved away the conference file. Her lunch was waiting for her in the small refrigerator in her bookcase, but she was in no hurry to eat. She would have liked to take lunch on a bench out in the fresh air, but knew she'd never get any work done this afternoon if she did.

There was a polite knock at her door. At her call, the door opened and Dak sauntered back in. "I thought I'd join you for lunch so we could finish our discussion."

"Lunch? Sorry. All I have is an apple and a diet soda. It's not enough for the both of us."

"Don't worry. I brought my own." He drew up a chair and dropped a brown paper sack on her desk. "I thought we could tie up any loose ends while we eat."

Katie watched in silence as he rummaged through the paper bag and withdrew a ham sandwich, pickle, a small container of potato salad, a cold drink and a package of two chocolate cupcakes with white frosting on top. "Is that all you brought?" she asked facetiously, jealous of his hearty lunch and his lithe figure.

"You said you were dieting. Of course," he added with a smile, "I could be persuaded to share the cupcakes."

She tore her eyes away from the food he'd lined up neatly on the desk. "No, thanks. If I ate that much at lunchtime, I'd be ready for a nap for the rest of the afternoon."

"I'll have to remember that."

He raised an eyebrow and, to Katie's chagrin, smiled that crooked smile of his. She felt her ears burn. "If you're going to make innuendos, I'll have to ask you to leave."

"Innuendos? I can't imagine what you're talking about. I'm just storing away useful information about my fiancée's behavior for future reference."

"I'm not your fiancée! How many times do I have to tell you I'm already married!"

Two women from the secretarial pool, late leaving for lunch, paused to glance through Katie's open door. Giggling when they saw Dak inside the office, they whispered to each other and disappeared.

"Everyone in the building thinks we're a twosome, whether you want us to be or not." He bit into his sandwich and chewed with relish. "There's nothing more satisfying than having a well-laid script go according to plan, is there?"

"Your plans, you mean," said Katie, biting into her tart apple.

"Now, now, don't be bitter. After all, your idea did get you a honeymoon."

"I need another honeymoon like I need a hole in the head," Katie shot back. "The job was a lot simpler before you showed up."

"First honeymoon not too satisfactory?" He casually ignored her answering frown. "As for me, I'm looking forward to a change of pace." He went to work on the potato salad and pickle. "This is great! Picnics are fun, aren't they?"

"Yeah, sure."

They ate silently. Finished with her apple, Katie couldn't help glancing over at the chocolate cupcake. Even though she was a lifetime member of Chocoholics Anonymous, she could feel her taste buds crying for satisfaction.

She blinked when her gaze met his. As though he'd read her thoughts, he silently undid the twin cupcake wrapper, took one cupcake for himself and slowly slid the other toward her.

"No, thanks. I wouldn't dare," she said, not certain the treat was the only temptation he was offering her.

"Ah, come on. This could be part of the act. Pretend we're celebrating our engagement."

She shook her head. Pretending to be engaged to him while claiming she was married to another man was something she wasn't sure she could handle.

"One bite?"

She resolutely put her hands in her lap. "I can't afford one bite. Trust me, I know."

"Okay. If a chocolate cupcake won't do for a celebration, how about this?"

Katie's eyes grew wide as Dak rummaged in his paper bag and drew out a slender circle of gold topped with a brilliant diamond. When he dusted bread crumbs off the ring, she asked, "Good heavens, do you have a box of Cracker Jacks in there?"

"Not exactly. I was passing a five-and-ten and dropped in. I thought an engagement ring was the right thing at a time like this."

"Delivered in a brown bag?"

"Why not?" He shrugged off the question. "I may have gotten a little carried away. I didn't want anyone to know what I was bringing in before you did. Besides, I wanted it to be a surprise."

"It's a surprise, all right." She examined the ring he handed her. "You've gotten it all yucky," she said as she picked at a tiny bread crumb and held the ring up to the sunlight. The diamond's blue and white hues sparkled in the sun. If it wasn't real, it was a mighty close facsimile.

She handed the ring back. "Sorry, I have one of my own at home. Better save it for your real bride."

Dak eyed her thoughtfully as he nibbled the waves of white icing from his cupcake and relished each bite. She didn't know it yet, but he was willing to bet that he would turn out to be as real a husband as Katie was going to get. He saw a flush come over her face and wondered just what there was about a chocolate cupcake that could make her respond that way.

Chapter Three

Nervously checking her watch, Katie glanced around the outer office of the Harrington Agency. She hoped the interview would be short and an appropriate "husband" would be available for hire in time for her to catch the noon flight back to Los Angeles from San Francisco. She'd taken only half a day off.

"Miss O'Connor?"

"Yes." Katie rose and entered the inner office. "Thank you for seeing me on such short notice."

"No problem," the smiling woman said as she motioned Katie to a comfortable chair in front of her desk. "I'm Rachel Harrington. Please call me 'Rachel.' From our phone conversation about why you need a temporary husband, I can understand your urgency. When did you say this meeting is going to take place?"

Katie bit the inside of her lower lip. "Next week. Miss Harr—Rachel. What I told you over the phone has to be kept in the strictest confidence."

"Of course, Miss O'Connor. Our agency is known for its discretion. That's why we're so successful. Now," she said briskly, "I've pulled together some photographs and résumés for you to look at. After you've made your choice, I'll arrange for an interview.''

"Oh no!" Katie exclaimed in dismay. If anyone discovered what she was up to, she'd wind up in deep trouble. "I won't have time to come back. I can't afford to have anyone find out that I came here in the first place. I'm perfectly willing to trust your judgment.''

Rachel crooked one eyebrow. "Are you certain you don't want to interview the gentleman? After all, you plan on spending a week with him.''

"I'm sure. That is, I'd prefer to let you be the judge.''

"It's highly irregular.'' Rachel glanced at the brass clock on the wall, as if weighing several consequences of Katie's urgency. "I guess it will be all right this time,'' she said finally. "But I will have to have you sign a waiver absolving the agency of any blame if you're unhappy in our choice.''

Rachel opened the portfolio and turned it toward Katie. "There are three men available for the time period you need—Lance Colbert, Steve Dana and Alex Diamond.''

Katie studied the glossy photos, turned them over and read the résumés pasted on the back. Colbert looked a little too old and Alex Diamond looked too much like an old boyfriend who'd been a heel. Steve Dana, she thought uneasily, reminded her of Dak, but he was the only choice left to her.

"This one will do, Rachel,'' Katie said as she handed her Dana's picture. "Now, let me be clear. I'm not looking for...''

Rachel's eyes flashed in understanding. "Be assured that our husbands are in name only.''

Katie sighed. Was that really what she wanted in her life?

As SHE DROVE to the Tickle Pink Inn, Katie reflected that Steve Dana, sitting next to her, had everything a woman could ask for in a husband: good looks, laughing eyes and a way of eyeing at a woman that made her pulse beat faster and her heart do tricks. Just her luck. What kind of insurance was he going to be if all he did was remind her of the man who made her blood boil—and her body ache?

It was her own fault that she was going to have to put up with Steve for a week. Had she, subconsciously, wanted him to resemble Dak, be like him? Rachel Harrington had assured her that Steve was an extremely likable escort and came well recommended. Well, she thought as she glanced over at her husband, she certainly had been right.

"Now, remember," Katie reminded him, "we're newlyweds and we're supposed to be crazy about each other. Okay?"

When the tall, dark, athletic man seated beside her sighed, she realized it wasn't the first time she'd laid out the requirements of his role. But she was nervous and wanted to get everything right.

"You know, Miss O'Connor, I'm a TV actor by profession. Between jobs right now, sure, or I wouldn't have hired myself out as a 'husband.' But this isn't what I intend to do with my life. I'm a damn good actor, and I'm going to make it big someday. Until then, don't worry about a thing. This job is a piece of cake."

Piece of cake. Katie wished she could be sure of that.

She carefully maneuvered her new BMW into a shaded parking spot in the Tickle Pink Inn's landscaped parking lot. A month old, the car was the love of her life and new enough to keep her from relaxing as she'd carefully driven up Highway 101 to the inn. That was the trouble with new cars, she thought ruefully, the first dent is the hardest to bear. That and the high monthly car payments.

Reminded again that her paycheck might depend on the success of the conference, Katie mentally ran through her proposed masquerade. She couldn't find a single flaw. With a bit of luck, she'd get through the week without a problem.

"I'll send out a bellhop to bring in the luggage," she told Steve as she handed him the car keys and gathered her purse and briefcase. "Meet you inside."

"Sure thing, Miss O'Connor. Say, by the way," he yelled after her. "Since we're supposed to be newlyweds I think it's a good idea if I call you 'Katie,' right? I'll have to remember that." Steve laughed cheerfully as he went around to the back of the car and opened the trunk.

Katie could hear him whistling as she entered the cool darkness of the inn. *She'd* have to remember to remind Steve not to get carried away by the role he was playing, that there were limits to their relationship.

It took a moment for her eyes to adjust to the soft lighting inside the reception room. A beaming Mrs. Fraser rose from her desk and bustled toward her.

"Hello again, Mrs. Smith. How nice to have you back here for your honeymoon! It's a shame you had to drive up by yourself, but your husband explained that you were detained by business. How was the wedding, dear? I'm sure you made a beautiful bride, and that handsome husband of yours! What a picture the two of you must have made.''

The only words Katie heard in the barrage of sound were "Mrs. Smith." Mrs. Fraser had called her that before, but she'd dismissed it as a bad joke that Dak had instigated to get on her nerves. Now it sounded as if it hadn't been a joke, after all. Her forced smile froze on her lips. ''What did you call me?''

''Mrs. Fraser called you Mrs. Smith, but I don't think you really expect her to be so formal, do you, darling? Why don't you call Katie by her given name, Mrs. F.?''

A firm hand grasped Katie's elbow and drew her against an unresisting hard body.

''I worried about you, my sweet. Next time, we drive together.''

Katie opened her mouth to protest.

''Don't even think about it,'' a cold voice murmured against her ear. ''Not a word. We'll talk later.''

''Here's an extra key for you, Katie. I've already given one to your husband.'' Mrs. Fraser smiled coyly at Dak. ''Suite 105, just as I promised.''

Katie hesitated.

''Take it, darling,'' Dak ordered softly.

Katie reached for the keys.

''Everyone else has arrived and is busy getting settled in. Now that your wife is here, Dak, I'm sure you'll want to, too. I'll have her bags sent right to your room.''

''Okay, Katie, love. I'm all yours. Have you registered yet? What's our room number?'' Steve Dana's deep, sensuous voice sounded behind Katie.

Mrs. Fraser's mouth fell open in shock as she took in the tall, good-looking actor. "Who are you and what was that you called Mrs. Smith?"

Steve came to a stop and looked around him. "Who's Mrs. Smith?"

Katie felt Dak's arm tighten around her in warning. She cleared her throat, but her voice still came out more like a squawk. "Mrs. Fraser, this is Steve Dana."

"My goodness!" The manager's eyes widened as she tore her gaze away from Steve and back to Katie. "I think I've seen this man on the soaps. What is he doing here and why is he calling you his love?"

Never missing a step in a scenario he'd learned by heart, Steve answered for Katie. "I'm Katie's husband. We're on our honeymoon." He looked at Katie for approval.

"Steve?" Under the pretext of nuzzling her throat, Dak said quietly, freezing the rest of Katie's introduction, "I thought your husband's name was Ken?"

"I, that is, I . . ."

"Don't pay any attention to Steve." Dak hugged Katie to him and laughed to cover her confusion. "He's Katie's brother and likes to kid around. Steve's visiting from out of town. We thought he might like to see the California coast so we brought him along. You don't mind do you?"

"Well, bringing along a guest on a honeymoon is a bit unusual, I must say." Mrs. Fraser eyed Steve with disapproval. "In fact, it's never happened before. However, there *is* a small cottage out on the grounds that we use when we're completely booked, as we are now."

"Great." Dak grinned. "Under the circumstances, you don't mind leaving us alone, do you, brother-in-law? We'll be by to see you later. Right, Katie?"

Obviously steeped in theatrical training, Steve politely waited for his cue as the script abruptly changed on him.

Katie could hardly meet his eyes. She tried to think of a way out of the trap Dak had set for her, but her mind was a wasteland. All she could come up with was that Steve must believe she was out of her mind, or at least close to it. Why else would she have hired him to play her husband when she apparently already had one of her own? The next move was up to her.

The back of Dak's hand caressed her cheek, then the side of her lips, urging a response.

"The cottage sounds wonderful, Steve," she finally managed. "Why don't you take it, and I'll come over to visit with you as soon as I can?"

The pressure of Dak's hand eased.

"Sure, take the cottage, Steve. But don't plan on waiting for us. I haven't had a chance to greet my new wife properly."

She could feel a flush rise over her at Dak's not-so-subtle reminder of the role he intended to play. Gazing mutely at the man she'd hired to be her husband, she mouthed the word "Later."

"Why not?" Steve shrugged, lifted his suitcase and gallantly gestured for Mrs. Fraser to precede him. "After you, ma'am."

"Do tell me all about Reilly in *Tomorrow Is Forever*, Mr. Dana. I'm an avid fan of his. Is it true that..." Her voice faded as she led the way through the French doors and out onto the patio.

"What do you think you can accomplish by keeping me from registering with my own husband?" Katie demanded as she struggled out of Dak's grasp.

"Husband, Katie? You've got it all wrong. I prefer to think I'm saving you from yourself."

"Saving me from— You must be out of your mind!"

"Come on, Katie O'Connor. You're no more married than I am, and you and I both know it."

"How would you know!" Hands balled into fists, she looked ready to attack.

"Simple. You weren't married when you hired on at Toyland, were you?"

"No. What's that got to do with it?"

"I happen to know that you haven't had your personnel file updated since then." Victory was sweet, Dak thought as he watched the light dawn on her face. "You would have found out that under California community-property laws, your husband has to sign away his spousal rights, even if you intended to keep your marriage a secret. Especially if you're going to continue using your own name on insurance and tax documents. Your file doesn't reflect any waivers signed by *Ken.*"

When Katie narrowed her eyes and opened her mouth, he made a show of apologizing. "Oh, I'm sorry, signed by *Steve,* or whatever his latest name is. I don't know what you had in mind by bringing a fake husband along, but I intend to find out. As a matter of fact, there are a few other interesting details buried in your file that I intend to clear up."

Katie gasped. When her face turned white, Dak checked himself. He hadn't wanted to scare the daylights out of her, only teach her a lesson, show her she didn't fool him for a minute. But maybe he was over-doing it. "The rest of this conversation had best be said privately. You never know who's listening." He took her arm. "Come on, suite 105 awaits us, Mrs. Smith."

She kept her silence until the door of their suite closed behind her. Then she swung on him.

"This reeks of blackmail! Just what is it you want from me?"

For the first time since he'd started checking up on Katie, Dak realized he didn't know exactly what he did want from her. To get even with her for usurping his territory? To salve his ego? Or because her body language intrigued him and he liked the way her mind worked? Especially when she was fighting mad. He definitely, he had to admit, wanted to have an excuse to keep her around. He settled for the obvious. "Nothing more than to be your husband for the con-ference."

"Why, for heaven's sakes? We can't even stand each other!" Katie knew she'd been found out, but she wasn't going to go gently into his arms. Not even when there was something about him that, under different circumstances, would have taken her there. The man had too much sex appeal.

"For security reasons, of course. It's my job to make certain no strangers get that close to the Toy-land employees. Who knows what this guy you brought up here might hear and what he might do with the information!"

"Good Lord! Steve Dana is harmless," Katie said helplessly. "Listening to you, a person would think there are spies coming out of the woodwork. Rachel

Harrington assured me he doesn't know a thing about toys, let alone Toyland."

"Rachel Harrington?" Dak frowned. "Who else is in on this?"

Katie dropped her things onto the coffee table. Dak may have her dead to rights, but she didn't have to bare her soul to him. She wasn't going to tell him about the Harrington Agency and make herself look like a complete fool. Besides, she didn't know enough about him to trust what he might do with the truth. It might even cost her her job.

"You're paranoid. You're worse than Neil Gibson. You're two of a kind." Hands on her hips, she let her frustration get the better of her. "Get this straight once and for all. There is nothing going on and there's no one else in on this! Whatever you think *this* is!" she said in disgust.

"So you say, lady. But just remember I'm not going to let up on you until I find out what you're up to! In the meantime, I'll just have to wait and see, won't I?"

Katie threw up her hands in despair and gazed around her at the lush setting she'd envied only a few days ago. Today the suite looked more like a prison and Dak Smith her jailer. If she had only guessed at the way things would turn out and how her hormones would quiver whenever he was around, she would never have suggested a honeymoon inn as a conference site.

"I'll have to have a quiet word with Mrs. F." she heard Dak remark. "I'm not sure she bought the story that Dana is your brother. There's your reputation to consider."

"*My* reputation?"

"Dana said you were married and were going to share a room. We don't know who else he told. Maybe even the bellhop." He frowned and paced the carpet. "That would give you two husbands, in case you can't count. Mrs. F. is friendly and emotional, but she's no dummy. When she's had time to think about it, she'll be asking questions and putting one and one together. I'll have to figure out what to do about it."

Katie jumped to her feet. "What *I'm* going to do is take a long, hot bath. And while I'm at it, you'd better figure out where you're going to sleep. There's a king-size bed in the next room that's only big enough for *one* of us. And for your information, I'm it!"

He stopped his pacing and studied her thoughtfully. Now that she was ready to accept him as her husband, things would be a lot easier for him. But he'd keep an eye on her just the same. "Good. I'm glad to see you're going to make the best of things. At least you have the good sense to know when you're licked."

"Who says I'm licked?" Katie paused at the bedroom door, ready to do battle.

"You've agreed to go along with me, haven't you? That proves I've been right about you. I still think you're up to something, though, and I'm going to find out what it is. In the meantime, I expect you to behave yourself and stay out of my job. And to act like my wife."

"Wrong, Mr. Smith. We may have to work together, but I'll never behave as if I'm your 'wife.' Not even a make-believe one. As for staying out of your territory, you tend to yours and I'll handle mine."

She slid open the bedroom door and closed it behind her with a bang.

Dak shrugged and wandered over to the liquor cart. The ice bucket was full—sliced fresh lemons and limes were in a shallow container resting on a bed of shaved ice. A note from the management bade him welcome and invited him to help himself. Dinner would be served informally in the garden restaurant at eight. He shed his jacket, loosened his tie and took off his shoes. Drink in hand, he collapsed in the deep cushions of the couch and sank back to survey the sleeping arrangements.

The bedroom was out. Not that he'd thought that far ahead until now. The way Katie was acting he'd be a fool even to think of sharing it with her, although the idea did have a certain appeal. Still, he reasoned, he had to keep his clothes in the closet and his personal items in the bathroom or the help would suspect something was wrong. He grinned as he contemplated Katie's reaction when she discovered his clothes hanging in the closet and his underwear and socks in the dresser drawers next to hers. As for his toothbrush and shaving kit, they would probably blow her mind when she found them in the bathroom.

One idle thought led to another as he listened to the sounds coming from the bathroom. He visualized her luxuriating in bath bubbles up to her chin in the combination Jacuzzi and bathtub large enough for two. The scent of honeysuckle bubble bath wafted through the slats in the sliding door. He could hear the hard sound of a fist splashing against the water and Katie talking to herself. It didn't take much imagination on his part to know she was using the water as a punching bag, or that her conversation was a blistering attack directed at him.

Nor did he have any trouble visualizing the scented bubbles against her creamy skin. Or the way she would have pinned up her silken auburn hair, or the drops of water sliding down her slender throat to her lush breasts, a path his fingers suddenly ached to follow.

So, he thought as he downed his drink and shifted uncomfortably, he obviously hadn't had enough of her type, after all. Every man had an Achilles' heel, and it appeared that strong redheads were his.

HE'D SHOWERED, shaved and was changing into clean clothing, when he heard a gasp. Wearing only a horrified look, Katie stood in the doorway. Averting his gaze, like the gentleman he wanted to think he was, Dak smothered a grin and tossed her the damp white robe he'd used. "Here, put this on. Not that I mind seeing you in your birthday suit, but I think you might when you realize what you're not wearing."

"What are you doing in here?" Katie clutched the robe to her chest and glared at him.

"The obvious, Mrs. Smith. Getting dressed for dinner."

"You could at least have had the decency to let me know that you intended to shower," she shot back, seemingly oblivious to the fact he had called her "Mrs. Smith," and that she was still largely uncovered and clothed only in her dignity. "I would have at least had the chance to put on a robe."

"You were sleeping so beautifully, I didn't have the heart to awaken you." Not that he hadn't been tempted, he thought ruefully as he eyed her flushed breasts and pink shoulders, but he wasn't prepared for the consequences. Not just yet, anyway.

Her face turned crimson. "You watched me while I was taking a nap?" she whispered. "What kind of a man are you? A voyeur?"

"Lucky for you, the kind of a man who can resist temptation, dear wife." Half-dressed, he slowly inspected her from the top of her head to her manicured toes, met her eyes and sighed. "And believe me, it wasn't easy."

He ignored her indignant gasp, pulled on a white crew-neck knit shirt and tucked it into his jeans. "By the way, tonight's dinner is casual. But I think it would be a good idea if you planned on wearing a few more things than you have on right now. Your reputation is already shaky enough."

He edged his way past her in time to avoid being hit by the damp robe, but not before brushing against a soft, bare shoulder. Behind him he heard a furious groan.

"I hope you're enjoying yourself!"

"Oh, I am. I most definitely am."

WHEN KATIE CAME out of the bedroom, she was wearing celery-colored palazzo pants, a sheer blouse and a crocheted vest to match. A silver chain that circled her slim waist tinkled as she walked. She carried a small silver mesh clutch in her hand. Beige sandals covered her freshly manicured toes. Lovely to look at, he thought as he admired her appearance. No, she was more than that. Positively breathtaking. "Very nice," he said, "but there's still something missing."

She frowned, moved to a full-length mirror that hung on one wall and carefully examined her image. "I can't see that I've missed anything."

Dak took a small velvet box out of his pocket and joined her in front of the mirror. "All brides should wear engagement and wedding rings, especially newlyweds," he said as he took her unresisting left hand and gently slid two rings onto her finger. "Not a crumb, this time. I was very careful to keep them clean."

Katie fingered the sparkling engagement ring and its matching wedding band. "You were awfully sure of yourself, weren't you?"

For a moment, he thought she was going to take the rings off her finger.

"Truce?" He covered her fingers with his. Her hand was soft in the way a woman's should be, he thought as he gently rubbed her skin. And warm the way a woman's hand should be. When she hesitated, he quietly added, "Forget our personal disagreement. It would be a good idea to wear the rings. They come with the territory. At least until the conference is over?"

She took a deep breath, considered his hand for what seemed to him an eternity, before she finally agreed.

"Truce, but only until the conference is over."

"And Steve?" he prompted. "You'll go along with my story?"

"I suppose I have to." She took another deep breath. "But don't think for a moment that I'm going to—"

"Hush," Dak said softly, anticipating what she was about to add. So it was going to be hands off, was it? Not if he had anything to say about it.

"One more thing, Katie. If I remember correctly, this goes with the occasion." When she looked inquiringly up at him, he put a forefinger under her chin and lifted her face to his. Before she could protest, he bent and kissed her cheek, her lips. It was not enough to satisfy the desire that flowed through him, but just enough to get the taste of her he'd been aching for ever since he'd seen her asleep.

When he finally raised his head, and could see their reflection in the mirror, it was in time to see Katie's hands start to rise to encircle his neck, hesitate, then fall away. So, he thought in pleased surprise, she must feel something for him, too.

Katie knew he was only kidding, teasing, maybe even taunting her. She remembered his earlier bitter words: marriage held no appeal for him. Not even a pretend one, and especially to her. This business of putting rings on her finger was only part of the game. Even so, there had been a certain charm about him when he'd lifted her chin and kissed her. A charm strong enough to make her momentarily forget they weren't lovers, not even friends.

She'd believed, not wanting to think, even as the response to his kiss remained within her, that he was being humorous. She might have forgiven him his amusement, if only she could be sure he was laughing with her, not at her. She remembered someone telling her that people didn't tease you unless they liked you. Dak had never shown that he liked her, let alone cared for her. She squared her shoulders, cast him a brief, uncertain glance and made for the door, leaving him standing in front of the mirror.

Whatever Katie O'Connor had intended, Dak thought with a pang of regret, she'd changed her mind. Too bad. She'd felt so good in his arms, so soft, so silky. He wanted more.

He hurried to catch up with her and open the door. He inhaled her honeysuckle scent as she passed, and put behind him the temptation to pull her back into the room, hold her close and kiss her again. And this time, to do a thorough job of it.

Until he remembered that she was a desirable woman, all right, but she'd proved she couldn't be trusted.

Chapter Four

Soft moonlight, enhanced by the muted colors of Chinese lanterns hanging from a latticed ceiling, cast a romantic glow over the garden terrace. Potted tropical plants and masses of spring daisies, pink and white geraniums, lavender petunias and pastel roses ringed the terrace. The soft sea breeze that blew from the sea mingled with the scent of jasmine. In one corner of the dining terrace, a pianist lovingly caressed ivory keys, softly singing the love song from the *"Phantom."*

"So, this is what honeymoons are made of," Dak commented as they arrived to join the other Toyland attendees for dinner. "Nice, if you like this sort of thing."

"Tell me why I'm not surprised you're so cynical, even about something as lovely as this," Katie answered. "I hope you treated your ex-wife better than this on your honeymoon."

"Never had a honeymoon," he commented matter-of-factly. "We were too busy arguing."

"Arguing, on a honeymoon?"

"Unfortunately, yes. I wanted to surprise my wife, so I had my travel agent plan a special honeymoon to Jamaica. But, naive me, my ex-wife had her own ideas about where she wanted to spend a honeymoon. We wound up staying home.''

"It seems to me that you should have consulted her instead of your travel agent.'' As Katie studied Dak, she realized what had been behind his bitter remarks about honeymoons. And it wasn't all because of her planning the conference at the Tickle Pink Inn. If any man had reason to be cynical about romance, it was Dak. He may have unwittingly caused his problem, but he had no right to take it out on her. "So that's why you were upset at my arranging to have this meeting in a honeymoon hotel.''

"Don't let it worry you. It wasn't a marriage made in heaven, anyway. And as for this setup—'' he glanced around with a bland expression ''—I still think this is a lamebrain idea.'' He took her arm and gestured to the bar, where the Toyland group stood socializing. "Let's go. Everyone's waiting for us. Now, don't forget—we're in love.''

"When pigs fly,'' Katie muttered, and gave him a sweet smile.

"Why is it I have this feeling I should have passed on this honeymoon, too?'' Dak commented dryly as he urged her forward.

"You have only yourself to blame for wanting to be in charge all the time. Even now. But just remember, you needn't have bothered to claim me as your wife. *I* already had a husband.''

"Yeah, sure.''

She gazed around the crowded room and frowned. "I should have checked on Steve.''

"I already did, while you were getting dressed.''

Katie stopped in her tracks. "And?''

"He seemed to be perfectly happy talking about his acting career with Mrs. Fraser and her niece, Ellen. He won't be here tonight. The Frasers have invited him for dinner." He eyed her with grudging admiration. "I have to hand it to you for your innovative thinking. Interesting touch, finding someone to play the part of your husband. Who is this guy, a boyfriend?"

Katie's conscience stirred. She'd never admitted to hiring a husband, but on the other hand, she hadn't denied it, either. Poor Steve, abandoned and left to the tender mercies of the Frasers before he had a chance to display his acting talents. By now he must think she'd lost all her marbles, but good sport that he obviously seemed to be, he was probably taking it in his stride. At least he was playing to an appreciative audience, which was more than she was doing. And, as it was turning out, he was probably a lot happier than she was with Dak clinging to her. She'd have to find Steve and explain as soon as she could get away from her jailer.

Katie shuddered to think of what Gibson would do if he heard about her hiring someone to play her husband. As for Dak, she mentally kicked herself for giving in so fast and allowing him to have such power over her. But he had another think coming if he thought he could push her around without a fight.

"This sounds more and more like blackmail, Dak Smith. You might as well come out with it. Just what is it you want from me?"

Dak considered the question for only a split second before the answer came to him like a bolt out of the blue. *To hold you in my arms and taste the honey of your lips and silken skin. To find out if the desire that comes into your eyes when you think I'm not looking*

*is as real as I imagine it would be when I take you in
my arms. And, heaven help me, that I'm afraid to find
out.*

Instead of giving himself away, he caught her chin
in his hand and kissed the tip of her pert nose.

Mesmerized by the way her eyes darkened with desire and her breath quickened, he bent and kissed the
dimple at the corner of her mouth. "Just what do you
think I want?" he asked, understanding full well they
both knew exactly what he wanted.

"I haven't a clue," she whispered.

"Giving up so easily?" When she shook her head,
he kissed her lightly on the other cheek and murmured into her lips, "It's going to be a long week. It
would be a shame to let the nights go to waste."

Before she could land a cutting reply, he glanced
over her shoulder. "Don't look now, but everyone has
noticed us. Play it cool, darling."

"Ah, there you are, Dak. You're sure a sly one. Got
yourself married, did you? And to the cutest redhead
I ever did see." Bob Winslow, the head of Toyland's
sales division, strode over to meet them, his wife in
tow. "Since we missed the wedding, I guess now's my
chance to kiss the bride."

Before she could protest, Katie found herself enveloped in powerful arms, and dodged the lips that
smelled of tobacco and whiskey.

"Why has Dak been hiding you, young lady?"

"Hold up there, Bob. I'm not sure I'm ready to
share Katie's kisses with anyone." Laughing, Dak
pulled a dazed Katie out of Winslow's arms. "Remember you're on a honeymoon of your own and
your wife is watching. Give Nora a big kiss before she
feels left out of this celebration."

Amid general laughter, Winslow grabbed his wife and repeated his performance.

"Dak, it was so nice of the company to give us all a second honeymoon," Nora Winslow enthused when her husband let her loose. The motherly woman in an uninspired gray lounge suit patted her hair back into place and beamed at Dak. "Inspired by your own recent marriage, was it?"

"You bet," he said with a broad smile on his face, "but you can thank my wife. It was all her idea, wasn't it, Katie?"

"So sweet!" Nora gushed, beaming at Katie as if she were a favorite granddaughter.

"Come on, honey." Dak accepted congratulations as he drew Katie to the bar. "Let me introduce you to the rest of the gang."

In short order, Katie began to match the women's faces and names with the men she'd been introduced to when she'd gotten her promotion five months earlier. There was Patrick Moriarity, director of manufacturing, and his Molly; Hal Martin, the head engineer, and his wife, Elaine; more than middle-aged Richard Lowe, head of advertising, and his shy young wife, Mary.

"Cynthia," Dak called, beckoning to a couple arguing in the background. "I'd like you to meet my wife. Since it was her idea to hold the conference here, she's the one to see if you have any complaints. Katie, this is Cynthia Mason and her husband, Edward. As you probably already know, Cynthia is the head of the art department."

"We've spoken on the telephone," Cynthia acknowledged, a frown creasing her forehead as her husband eyed Katie with interest. "Edward, put your eyes back in their sockets. Katie is a newlywed, and impervious to your charms."

"Better believe it, and she's all mine," Dak laughed as he kissed the back of Katie's hand. "Aren't you, sweetheart?"

"You'll have to excuse Edward. He thinks he's a gift to women." Cynthia Mason's voice and cold look didn't seem to bother her pompous husband.

Mason laughed. "Haven't had any complaints yet," he said as he continued to ogle Katie. "Nice going, Dak."

Dak wanted to punch the obnoxious smile off Mason's face. The damn fool had no right to look at Katie that way. Nor, for that matter, did any other man. Surprised at the burst of jealousy that shot through him, Dak put her behind him and gestured to the dining tables, which were quickly filling up with other guests.

"Now, if you folks are ready for dinner, shall we?" Dak led the way to pink and gray covered tables set with floral nosegays. Each table had a champagne bottle nesting in ice. In keeping with the honeymoon theme of the inn, each table was set for two.

Out of the corner of her eye, Katie could see the Masons still arguing. "Doesn't look as if they are enjoying their second honeymoon, does it?" she whispered.

"Cynthia is a shrew, and not only up here. She's a pain and Mason deserves her," Dak said dryly. "They're made for each other. It's been my experience that all Cynthias are shrews."

"Cynthia? Let me guess, your ex-wife?"

"Especially my ex-wife."

The edge in his voice spoke of pain. Katie remembered how he'd refused to go along as her husband when Neil Gibson had first suggested it, and the bitterness in his voice when he'd spoken of his disastrous honeymoon. No wonder he'd been unwilling to play at being married, even if only for a short time. In spite of recalling she was the fake wife he'd initially rejected, she found herself strangely sympathetic.

She noticed the hard look come back into his eyes, the way his lips tightened. Even so, he was still the type of man most women dream about... and she was no exception.

She couldn't imagine any female letting him go. Dakota Smith was the kind of a man she'd might have liked, and perhaps, in a another lifetime, even more.

"You have to admit this is a lovely place for Toyland's affair," she commented as they were seated.

"Affair?" Unfolding his napkin, Dak regarded her with a sardonic smile. "Is that how you see this business conference? An affair?"

"Of course." When he raised an eyebrow, Katie did a double take. "Now, just a minute. Do you have to turn everything into a sexual innuendo? Is that all you ever think about?"

"Lately." He poured champagne into her glass and winked at her. "Anyway, I'm willing to bet that it's been on your mind, too. Come on, be honest enough to admit it."

"Keep your mind on the job you're here for," Katie answered, appalled at the ease with which he'd read her mind. "You take care of security and pretending to be my husband and I'll do the rest!"

"Oh, I will." He toasted her with his full glass. "I most certainly will, Katie my love."

She squirmed in her chair. The promise in his voice was precisely what she was afraid of. How far did he plan on taking this game? As the piano was joined by a flute and a cello, she was taken aback to realize there was an invitation in Dak's eyes. This time he was doing more than just laughing at her, but strangely enough the suggestive tone of his voice no longer seemed to bother her.

He could be patronizing, she thought as she considered him, but threatening, no. She was onto him now. Beneath that tough exterior he was a flesh-and-blood man just like the rest. After sparring with five brothers for most of her life, she was sure she could handle anything Dak could dish out.

"Dare to dance?"

She started to refuse—changed her mind. He had a twinkle in his eye that showed he was aware she was attracted to him. She was, although she was more afraid of herself than him. After watching other honeymooners dancing cheek to cheek for the past half hour, she'd been thinking about being held against his broad chest, having his strong arms around her, holding her close.

"Yes, thank you. It *is* what everyone expects honeymooners to do, isn't it?" she said casually, hoping she hid her anticipation. "But I want to warn you, I have two left feet. I don't dance very well."

"That's okay. I'll teach you." In lithe movements, he came around the table, led her to the dance floor and took her in his arms.

Pretending to be a honeymooner, and maybe feeling just a little bit like one, Katie laid her check against his warm chest and let herself be enfolded in his reassuring arms. His solid strength, the light pressure of his hand on her back guided her and took her into a world she hadn't known existed before. She found herself following where he led as easily as if she'd been dancing all her life, and somehow she knew she'd never be able to dance this way with anyone else but him.

His heartbeat was strong and steady, his voice soft and mellow as he hummed along with the music. From his earlier cynical remarks, she would never have guessed he had music in his soul and could move so gracefully. But he did, and as he swept her along to the melody, she entered a different world in his arms.

Physically close to him for the first time, she felt the room, the other dancers fade away until there was only the two of them moving to the sound of the musicians in the background playing "I Will Always Love You." She closed her eyes, lost in the dreamworld the music and Dak's sheltering arms created around her. She fought the urge to move closer to him, to slide her fingers through the hair at his nape, to feel his rough skin against her cheek. Moved by the solid strength of the man who held her, she could have gone on dancing forever.

As the music ended, she looked up at Dak and at the enigmatic smile on his face.

"Happy, Mrs. Smith?"

Mrs. Smith! Suddenly a dose of reality swept over her and put the dream to rest. With the Toyland executives looking on, she realized he was acting a part as surely as Steve Dana had acted his. Roles they were all being paid to play.

In spite of his sultry suggestive smiles, the fact remained that Dak suspected her of some sort of evil intent.

"I'm going to find Steve," she said as the music started up again.

"I'll go with you."

"I'd rather you didn't. I'd prefer to be alone." When his eyes grew cold and the smile left his face, she fought the urge to take back her harsh words, to apologize for shattering the tenuous bond that had developed between them during the dance. Keeping her emotional distance was her only defense against his growing attraction for her.

"I intend to be right alongside you whenever you talk to him," Dak said quietly as he caught her by the arm. "At least until I've had a chance to check him out."

"This is ridiculous! You see a criminal behind every bush. Steve has nothing to do with Toyland. Now, let me go!"

"The hell you say." He gave a strange laugh, but loosened his grip. "People are watching us having a very public quarrel. My, my, how history repeats itself."

She looked around at curious eyes. Nora Winslow was smiling sadly and shaking her head in reproof. Cynthia Mason appeared smug and satisfied. Katie was afraid to check out the reaction of the others in the Toyland group. It was more than she could take.

"Let me go, or I'll scream and you'll have a lot more to explain than this," she said between clenched teeth. "I'll meet you later."

He released her so suddenly she staggered. She regarded him coldly and headed for the garden that surrounded the terrace. Behind her she heard surprised gasps and raised voices calling to Dak in the lull in the music. She was pleased. Now that he would be kept too busy to follow her, she could talk to Steve alone where no ears could overhear her.

The moon was high as she made her way through the landscaped grounds and along a cobblestone pathway strung with softly lit lanterns. Ahead, off to one side, she could make out a small Hansel and Gretel white-and-gray cottage. Glancing cautiously around her, she knocked on the door.

Steve Dana, shirt unbuttoned to his waist and combing tousled hair away from his forehead, opened the door on her third try. "Katie? What are you doing here?"

"Quick, let me in. I have to talk to you."

"Er... just a minute." He glanced behind him at a partially closed door and back to Katie. "Better let me put myself together first."

"Good heavens, don't be so modest." She pushed him aside. "We *are* supposed to be married, aren't we?"

"Gosh. Beats the hell out of me." He shrugged as he buttoned his shirt. "Are we?"

"I wanted to explain—" She broke off when she noticed Ellen Fraser straightening her blouse as she watched from the doorway of the adjoining room. Blushing, Katie apologized. "I didn't mean to..."

"I was just showing Ellen how we do love scenes on TV. Under the circumstances, I didn't think you'd care."

"Don't worry, Mrs. Smith, or is it Mrs. Dana? I'm just leaving." Ellen smiled archly and walked to the door. "I'll be back for acting lessons another time. Bye-bye, Steve."

Katie waited until Ellen had disappeared before turning back to her hired husband. Taking in his unabashed grin, she silently railed at the fate that filled her existence with men too sensually handsome for their own good, and hers.

"Honestly, I didn't mean to break up anything. I just wanted to make certain you were okay and to tell you that I'd be back later, as soon as Dak falls asleep."

She tried to explain the situation without giving too much away. The less Steve knew, the better it would be for him. Especially if Dak kept his promise to question him later. "I'll be back as soon as I can to stay the night. I don't intend to spend a single night with that man. I don't trust him."

"This is the damnedest script I ever heard of," Steve finally managed, "but you're the boss and you're paying me to stick around. I still can't figure out why you needed to call the Harrington Agency. Or why you're so set on avoiding the man who calls himself your husband. But, if that's what you want, I'll leave the door open for you."

"Thanks for understanding. See you later." She wasn't ready to admit she'd hired a husband to avoid giving Dak any satisfaction. Or that she wanted Steve to remain so that Dak wouldn't get too close.

As Katie hurried along the walk, she was intercepted by an agitated Mrs. Fraser.

"Now, see here, Mrs. Smith. I can't allow this sort of thing at the Tickle Pink Inn. We have a well-established inn and an excellent reputation to consider. Such goings-on are absolutely not permissible."

Katie groaned. Ellen must have told her aunt enough to make the lady suspicious. "Honestly, Mrs. Fraser, it's not what you think."

"Save your breath, young lady. Your husband has already explained that you brought that man along to make Dak jealous and to keep him in line. And on a honeymoon? I wouldn't have believed it if I hadn't seen it with my own eyes!"

"You shouldn't believe a word Dak says, I tell you. There's more to this than I can explain at the moment."

"Humph! Dak told me you'd say something like that. Well, let me tell you, the only reason I'm not asking Mr. Dana to leave is that Ellen is quite taken by him. But let me tell you, poor Dak deserves more than this kind of shenanigans on his honeymoon. What kind of marriage do you think you're going to have if you carry on this way from the start?"

Katie knew when she was licked. Mrs. Fraser was clearly impressed enough with Dak not to listen to anything she had to say. "Good night," she murmured, backing away from the woman's accusing eyes.

She hurried around the building and into a side door to the inn. As she slipped inside, a shadowy figure moved forward.

"Mrs. Smith...Katie. I'm so glad I've bumped into you." Nora Winslow put her finger across her lips and motioned for silence. "I was just going out for a breath of fresh air," she whispered. "After witnessing your lovers' quarrel, I couldn't sleep for thinking about you and your husband."

"That's sweet of you, Mrs. Winslow. But it really wasn't a quarrel. It was just a misunderstanding."

"I've been married for thirty-five years, my dear, and to a man who acts first and thinks afterward. So I know that misunderstandings can become serious if you don't settle them right away. Let me give you a bit of advice my own grandmother passed along to me when I was first married. Two heads that share the same pillow can settle anything, if you get my meaning?"

"Well, yes, I do." Katie choked back a hysterical urge to laugh. She was beyond the age of blushing at the idea of marital sex, but Mrs. Winslow *was* old enough to be her mother. Except that her own mother would never had spoken so freely or so frankly. "I'll try to remember that. And thank you for caring."

Katie escaped to the door of suite 105 before she let loose the giggle that had threatened her during her conversation with Mrs. Winslow. How many of the other Toyland attendees would be orchestrating her reconciliation with Dak before another day was over? she wondered as she tiptoed across the darkened suite.

Just as she reached the bedroom, the door slid back and Dak, clad only in pajama bottoms, stood in the doorway.

"Well, it's about time you came home."

He was too much! First, there had been Steve and a knowing Ellen, then the encounter with Mrs. Fraser and the stern lecture that had followed. Finally, Mrs. Winslow had been lying in wait to deliver a speech on marital relations. And now here was an irate, half-naked Dak to continue the comedy. All occurrences she would never have anticipated even if she'd tried, and ones that boggled even her literal mind. Normally slow to see humor unless someone explained the punch line to her, Katie, torn between the urge either to laugh or to cry, pushed past him, threw herself into a chair and burst into laughter.

Dak cautiously approached her. "Are you okay?"

She tried to explain in between the renewed bursts of laughter that bubbled up in her throat. But he was such an incongruous sight in his pajama bottoms and tousled hair she couldn't contain herself. Even the concern on his face sent her off again. He was treating her as a wayward wife, for goodness' sakes, just as if he were really her husband! Doubled up with the effort to catch her breath at a renewed onslaught of hiccups, she could only nod helplessly.

Dak eyed her warily and disappeared into the bathroom to bring her a glass of water. "Here, take a long drink. If that doesn't work, hold your breath and count to ten."

Katie took the glass in a shaking hand, managed a long swallow and, when the hiccups continued, counted to ten.

"There's one more cure my great-aunt Tilly used to use," he said as he leaned over and rubbed her earlobe. "Better?"

Moved by the unexpected touch of his fingers on her sensitive ears, Katie swallowed a hiccup. Seconds later, the hiccups resumed.

None of the age-old remedies seemed to help. "What are you doing in here?" she finally managed.

"Where did you think I'd be while you were out after midnight with your imposter husband?"

"My other fake husband, you mean," she said, giggling between hiccups, knowing she was giving something away, but too hysterical to stop. She was tempted to try again to tell him of the misadventures she'd experienced in the past hour, but the hiccups wouldn't stop.

He peered closely at her. "Have some more water."

"It's not working." She giggled uncontrollably into the half-filled glass of water.

"I have another remedy, if you're willing to try it."

Immediately, a vivid scene popped into her mind, of Dak taking her to bed and keeping her too occupied to think of the hiccups. The growing warmth in his eyes and a quirked eyebrow confirmed her suspicion. "Don't you even think about it!" she threatened, and burst into another involuntary bout of giggles.

"You've either had too much to drink or you're hysterical! What were you doing with that guy Dana besides drinking?"

The unexpected accusation shocked the hiccups out of her. Katie felt as though she'd been doused with a cold shower. "What was I doing? What was I doing? I'll tell you what I was doing, you nitwit, and then I'm going to punch you right in the nose. You're not one of my brothers or my husband. How dare you speak to me that way!"

She scrambled out of the chair, marched up to Dak and balled up her hands, ready to carry out her threat. Until a close look at his face stopped her hands in midair. "You're jealous!" she said, more in surprise than in anger.

"Jealous? Of you? Ridiculous!" Even as he spoke he realized she was right. His "wife" had hit the nail right on the head. Either he'd gotten carried away by the role he was playing, or he *was* actually jealous. First of Ed Mason and now of Steve Dana! He could dismiss Mason; the middle-aged dandy couldn't possibly appeal to Katie. But, heaven help him, he *was* jealous of his fake wife's make-believe husband!

Shocked, he stared at her. If the devil was a red-headed woman, as he had long suspected, she was standing in front of him!

Chapter Five

The couch was too hard and the night too long. Dak grunted his annoyance, turned over and narrowly missed falling off. He damned his own insistence on playing Katie's husband. Determined to make different sleeping arrangements before another day was through, he elbowed a narrow nest in a vain attempt to make himself more comfortable. He might have slept, but her accusation kept him from dozing off.

Jealous? Hell, no! He may have been guilty of an overreaction at finding her missing, but he *had* seen her go to bed earlier. Security was his business; any indications of a possible breach in that always heightened the flow of adrenaline in his system. His response to finding her gone in the dead of the night had merely been the instinctive response of a well-trained security man, he told himself. And he'd been right. If he hadn't watched her like a hawk, she might have been off doing something that could have given their ruse away. Worse yet, she might have gotten herself kidnapped.

Lord, but she found ways to get under his guard. And that innocent look of hers! She was as clever as a devil's daughter. He was paid to be concerned for her welfare, and still she had the nerve to call him jealous? Absolutely ridiculous. He slammed his head back against the pillow and hit wood. Dammit, he told himself as he drifted uncomfortably back to sleep; he didn't have a jealous bone in his body.

Behind the closed bedroom door, Katie was resolutely unmoved by Dak's groans and muttering. If he thought to win her sympathy, he had another think coming. Whatever discomfort he was going through, he'd brought it all on himself.

She waited until his breathing settled into a steady rhythm before she dressed in navy blue sweats and bound a scarf around her hair. It was well after two o'clock when she finally made her way across the living room and glanced cautiously to where Dak slept on the couch. He was out like a light, lying on his stomach and mumbling in his sleep. One hand trailed down to the floor. Out in the hall, she checked to see if anyone was prowling about, hugged her dark blue windbreaker closer and made for the side door.

The grounds were dimly lit, with only an occasional safety lantern illuminating the way. The windows of the cottage at the end of the walkway were dark. She knocked softly several times before turning the knob; the door was locked and there was no answer. Steve had either forgotten her or he was too busy to answer the door. Muttering her annoyance, she had started back to the main building, when the sound of a barking dog broke the stillness. Good heavens, she thought as she hurried through the night. The way things had been going, Mrs. Fraser would be up and checking the grounds before she reached safety. One more encounter and lecture was more than Katie could bear.

She unlocked the door to the suite, blinked when she saw the empty couch, then moved to the bedroom doorway. Dak had taken her place in the king-size bed and was fast asleep. He'd left her half the bed, but he was out of his mind if he thought she'd crawl into his tangled web. As far as she was concerned, bundling had gone out with the eighteenth century.

Just her luck, she thought as she made for the couch and, fully clothed, sank into its depths. The past twenty-four hours had to be lived to be believed. Even she found it hard to sort out. What had started out as a harmless masquerade using a hired husband had deteriorated into a slapstick comedy, with herself as the hapless heroine and Dak as the hero determined to save her from herself. That he thought she needed saving was one of the things about him that annoyed her the most. That and his patronizing attitude. Five brothers aside, she'd been taking care of herself for a long time, and she didn't need an egotistical security guard to tell her how to live.

Could she really keep up with this nonsense for the entire week? Not with Dak acting like a jealous husband, for Pete's sake. As for Steve Dana, she found it difficult to be angry at him. Freed from his husbandly role, he'd obviously found Ellen Fraser a bigger attraction than sheltering Katie for the night. Not that she blamed him. But she was going to have to insist he at least leave the cottage door unlocked tomorrow night.

She pulled the blanket under her chin and stretched her legs. Tomorrow promised to be a crazy day and her mind grew dizzy as she tried to figure out a way to keep three moves ahead of Dak.

"GOOD MORNING."

Dak's cheerful voice awakened her. Sunlight hit her eyes.

"Sleep well?"

"No," she muttered from beneath the pillow she'd put over her head to close out the sun, "and you know it. You were supposed to be sleeping out here on the couch. The bed was mine."

"Well, since no one was using the bed at one o'clock in the morning, I figured I might as well enjoy it," he answered as she turned over to face him. "As for sleeping on the couch—" his eyes swept over her with apparent interest "—better thee than me, sweetheart. You have the right body size for it. Besides, I had the strong impression you intended to spend the night in Dana's cottage, and that you might not be back."

"Spying on me?" Katie was still wiping sleep from her eyes when she sat up and noticed his satisfied smile. Instinctively, she pulled the top of the sweat suit down over her waist where it had inched up as she'd slept, exposing her middle. Heat suffused her as his eyes followed her hands.

"Nope. I already had inside information that Ellen Fraser and Dana were sharing *her* room. I figured I'd let you stew in your own juice while I got a good night's sleep."

"No wonder no one—" Katie broke off in mid-sentence. "How did you know Steve wouldn't be there?"

"It's my job to know everyone's whereabouts," he answered more than a little smugly as he pulled back the drapes. "Rise and shine, or you'll be late."

"I don't think I can," she muttered into her hands. "What time is it, anyway?"

"Seven-thirty. I've already showered, shaved and dressed, so the bathroom's all yours. Better hurry. Today is a workday, Mrs. Smith."

"Try to remember I'm not Mrs. Smith!"

"Suit yourself, but your daily agenda for the conference calls for Mrs. Smith to breakfast at eight and to start the meeting at nine."

"Why didn't you wake me sooner?" Katie scrambled off the couch and made for the bedroom, groaning as she stubbed her toe against a chair.

"You looked so cute sleeping in that getup," he called after her disappearing figure. "Dressed so that no one would know who you were in the dark, right? Didn't you forget your mask?"

The door slid shut with a bang.

Chuckling to himself at her pique, Dak folded the blanket and straightened the pillows on the couch. No way was he going to let the help know he and Katie had slept apart on their "honeymoon"! He looked ruefully at the bedroom doors; at the rate she kept banging them, he'd have to pay for their repair. Ah, those redheads, he thought, for the first time fondly. All spice. Enough to keep a man on his toes for the rest of his life.

He rummaged through the coffee service. There were three kinds of exotic coffee blends, tea and all the trimmings. Better than room service, under the circumstances. He plugged in the coffeepot. He didn't want any questioning glances until he had the blanket safely stashed in the bedroom and all evidence of separate beds erased.

After last night, he needed something black and strong to get him started. If he could only think of a way to keep Katie in their suite while they settled their differences. He started to open the door to tell her about the coffee, when he heard her speaking softly into the phone.

"McDuff?" There was a pause before he heard her resume her conversation. "No, I can't talk about it right now, but I'll call you again tomorrow morning."

McDuff? Who could the mysterious McDuff be? Or was it a code word, and if it was, what did it mean? And why couldn't she talk about it now? What was she concealing from him? His head spinning with questions, his antenna up, Dak backed away from the door. Whatever she was up to, she would bear watching. Maybe there was more to this feisty redhead than he'd bargained for.

By the time Katie joined him, Dak had made up his mind to stick to her like a second skin. Once they had the conference under way, he'd offer to act as an escort for her and the spouses while she kept them too busy to question what was going on. He scowled as he remembered that the philandering Ed Mason would probably be part of the contingent Katie would herd through the week. And that her "husband," Steve Dana, was still someone to deal with. Under the circumstances, he decided escorting Katie and her charges was definitely a job for a seasoned security expert like him.

"Still here?"

Dak put down his half-finished cup of coffee. "As a newly married man, where else would I..." His voice faded as he gazed at a transformed Katie. Her softly tailored two-piece silk pantsuit of forest green and pastel green blouse complemented her auburn hair, deepened the color of her emerald eyes. Hints of silver sparkled in her eyes, a reflection from the earrings and mesh necklace she wore at her slender neck. The scent of honeysuckle blossoms followed her. He glanced cautiously at her left hand as she pushed back an errant curl from her forehead. The rings he'd given her were still on her finger. Either she was a true professional or she wasn't as angry at him as she pretended. He nodded his approval. Katie O'Connor was a quick study. "Lovely, Mrs. Smith."

The half smile that had started to appear on her face at his compliment vanished when he called her "Mrs. Smith." She frowned and made for the door.

"Hold up a minute! Let me get this stuff put away before we go." Dak gathered the blanket and her shoes and took them into the bedroom.

"What was that all about?" Katie inquired as they left the suite. "Housekeeping part of your job, too?"

"Hardly, but keeping up the appearance of a happily married couple seems to be. What would the staff think if they knew we slept apart last night?"

With an audible sniff, Katie led the way to the cliff terrace, where breakfast waited.

"My dears!" Mrs. Winslow called from her table in front of the buffet. "We were about to give up on you."

Mrs. Winslow beckoned to Katie and whispered in her ear, "You look radiant this morning. Apparently you took my advice last night." When Katie appeared blank, Nora Winslow leaned over again and whispered in Katie's ear, "The same pillow, remember?"

Katie blushed to remember the well-meant advice. Keeping her eyes averted from Dak, she nodded. "I remembered. And yes, we both slept on the same pillow." As Nora patted her hand in approval, Katie felt no remorse for misleading her. She and Dak *had* shared the same pillow, even though it hadn't been at the same time or in the same bed.

"The schedule says we're golf widows today, so we've decided to go shopping in Carmel. Would you like to come along?"

"Thanks anyway. Later, perhaps." Katie's mind was occupied with the logistics of getting the meeting off to a good start and the need to keep the women and Ed Mason too busy to miss their spouses. "You go on ahead. I'll catch up with you in a while."

"Catch up where?" Carrying two glasses of chilled orange juice, Dak came up behind Katie and handed her a glass. "Here you go, sweetheart."

"Now, isn't that thoughtful," Nora gushed. "My own bear of a husband ate earlier and left for the golf course for an 8:00 start. And this is supposed to be our second honeymoon!" She laughed. "I guess he's too set in his ways to change, even for me."

"Nora's invited me to go along to Carmel to do some shopping," Katie explained. She wasn't happy about leaving the conferees to their own devices, but it was her job to act the social director of the conference.

"And you're going?" Dak asked Katie.

She bridled. From the tone of his voice, he wasn't asking. Maybe he was right. Gibson's instructions *had* been to keep an eye on the spouses and to keep them too busy to ask questions.

"Great," he continued cheerfully, "I'll have Mrs. Fraser line up someone to take you."

"Ellen Fraser has volunteered the inn's van, and she's even going to drive," Nora interjected. "Wasn't that thoughtful of her?"

When Steve and Ellen joined the group, Katie made a beeline for Steve. She had to talk to him about leaving the cottage door unlocked before another night passed. And to explain that Mrs. Fraser was suspicious. Dak caught her by the arm. "Cool it, Katie," he muttered. "Things are bad enough already. The bellhop thinks you're Dana's wife, and Mrs. Fraser thinks he's your boyfriend. I don't expect my introducing him as your brother will have put the matter to rest. Especially if you're going to be too friendly with him."

"And whom do I have to thank for that?" She shot back as she smiled brightly for the benefit of their audience. "I had everything under control until you decided to play the game your way." With a brief nod to Nora, she excused herself and went to Steve's side. She'd show Dak that he couldn't run her life.

"Hi, Katie!" Steve kissed her warmly on her cheek and threw his arm around her shoulders. "How's everything?"

"Not good enough," Katie mumbled with a black look in Dak's direction. Ignoring his obvious disapproval, she let Steve's arm remain around her. "Why did you lock the door to the cottage last night?"

Unabashed, Steve laughed. "You were kind of late, and I had a date."

"From what Steve's told me, you didn't need him anymore. Not with that gorgeous hunk over there claiming to be your husband. Of course," Ellen said as she glanced over at Dak and back to Steve, "I can understand why it's hard to choose between them. As for me, I favor Steve," she said as she grabbed his arm possessively. "Come on, honey, let's go get the van."

It took only a minute for Katie to decide that, in spite of Steve's compelling good looks and winning ways, she definitely preferred Dak. He was no actor trading on his sex appeal. And while he was annoying with his overbearing ways, she had to give him credit for doing his job as he saw it. He was also strong, capable and clearheaded. A man a woman could trust, depend on.

"Looks as if between two husbands, you can't keep one and can't stand the other," Dak commented dryly as he joined her. "I've decided to go along with you to Carmel. Come on, let's eat breakfast and get the meeting started. We can drive up later and catch up with the others. I really should stick around here, but..."

"Be my guest. You can stay. I'll be just fine without you." Katie eyed Dak. He looked every inch the part of a honeymooner in his casual sand-colored slacks and a fresh brown turtleneck shirt that set off his tanned complexion and sun-drenched brown hair. As Katie took in his lithe figure, his casual clothing, she felt both envious and overdressed.

"I'm going to check the conference room to make sure everything's ready." She glanced down at her attire, thinking that it was far too conservative for a day in Carmel. "Then I think I'll go back to the room to change into something more comfortable before we leave," she said. "Anyway, I seldom have anything more than juice and coffee in the mornings."

"Juice and coffee in the mornings, fruit and diet drinks for lunch," Dak said reflectively as his eyes roamed over her. "And what do you do at night?"

She felt a blush spread over her face when he quirked his eyebrows in mock surprise. Damn, she'd done it again: fed him a line that left her wide open to another of his sexual innuendos. "If it's food you're talking about, I have a well-balanced meal in the evening," she answered.

"Shame on you, Katie O'Connor." She cringed, but held her tongue when he laughed and added, "What else did you think I had in mind?"

DAK GLANCED over at Katie, whose auburn curls whipped in the wind as they drove northward to Carmel. She'd changed into hot pink palazzo pants, a matching T-shirt and a beige see-through sweater that didn't conceal the curve of her lush breasts. Her jewelry, except for her rings, was gone. Pink Keds were on her feet. If ever a woman looked more sexy and kissable, he thought with an appreciative second glance, he had yet to meet her.

The beauty of the drive from the Tickle Pink Inn to Carmel in Dak's convertible kept Katie from being annoyed at him. As they drove through a wooded area, she caught glimpses of the ocean and sandy beaches. She leaned her head back against the cushions and enjoyed the clean, salty air and the billowing clouds that drifted through a clear blue sky.

"If you don't mind a short detour, I'd like to show you something interesting."

"I'm always open to seeing something interesting, or hadn't you noticed," Katie replied saucily.

"I've noticed, all right," he replied. And he'd gleaned a lot more than that about her, too.

Dak turned off at a sign marking the way to Point Lobos Park. After paying a fee to the park ranger, he came to a stop at a parking lot at the edge of the cliffs, overlooking the ocean.

"Look over there, Katie." He pointed at the rocks where seals and otters slept in the sun. While they watched, two small otters slid into the water, chased each other, flipped over onto their backs and clapped their fins. "Listen," Dak said when the otters barked. "Sounds as if they're laughing, doesn't it?"

Fascinated, Katie could only watch and nod.

"If you like, we can walk down that pathway over there and look at the tide pools."

"Oh please," she answered. "I haven't done that since I was a kid."

"Then hop out, O ancient one." Dak glanced at his watch. "I figure we can spend half an hour at least."

"Want to go wading?" he asked when they reached the bottom of the cliff. "Take off your shoes and watch for broken shells." As Katie shucked off her Keds and displayed manicured toes, he smiled at her delight. All he'd done was indulge a wish he'd seen come across her face and she was acting as though he'd given her a special gift.

He took off his own shoes and socks and followed her while she happily collected small shells and colored rocks. Their toes touched once or twice in passing, leaving Dak to dream of feet touching under silken sheets. When they'd both bent over to pick up the same seashell, she bumped her head against his.

"Sorry," he said, watching her rub her forehead. "I didn't hurt you, did I?" He wanted to ask her if he could kiss her forehead to make it better, but didn't want to push his luck.

When it was time to leave, Katie said, "I wish we could stay longer."

"Another time. Today we're on Toyland's payroll." Would there be another time? he wondered, another day when he could devote twenty-four hours to exploring Katie's world? The idea was worth thinking about, but business first.

She looked at her sandy, wet feet. "Oh dear, I'm afraid I'm going to get sand in your car."

"Not to worry." He handed her his handkerchief. "When you dry off, you can use it to carry your collection."

When they reached the car, Katie glanced back at the ocean where otters still played. "I can't remember when I've had so much fun," she said wistfully.

"Stick with me and I'll show you how to have more fun."

Katie straightened and glanced sharply at the expression of studied innocence on Dak's face. "I'll bet!"

"Doing it again, Katie? Better take care."

She leaned back and counted to ten. Wasn't there anything she could say that didn't have a double meaning? Or that he wouldn't turn into one?

"Ever been to Carmel?" he asked, hoping to draw her back into conversation.

"No, but I've heard a lot about it."

"There's an art gallery that's a favorite of mine. I'd like to show it to you. After we eat lunch."

"Lunch? I told you I seldom—"

"You'll eat lunch today," he said firmly. "There's a health-food restaurant that serves a great low-cal chili. I told Ellen I'd meet them there at one." He went on to describe two kinds of beans drowning in onions, green peppers and tomatoes, liberally spiced with chili powder. "And they serve it with corn bread that leaves you crying for more."

"I wouldn't dare."

"Trust me. You'll love it." He drove down a side street until he found a vacant spot. "Grab a quarter out of my pants pocket for the parking meter, will you?"

When he felt the pressure of her searching fingers through the material on his thigh, he caught his breath. "On the other hand, maybe not. I'll get it for myself in a minute."

Katie snatched back her hand; their eyes locked. A faint smile crossed her face that told him she'd realized what was bothering him. And the look that came into her sparkling eyes revealed her pleasure at making him squirm.

"Lunch," he said firmly as he came around to let her out of the car. "And after lunch, the art gallery."

"We should be checking on the rest of the gang."

"They'll be here soon, if they're not here already. I gave Ellen the address. Anyway, at least they're too busy to notice what's going on back at the inn. After lunch, there's plenty here in town to keep them occupied for the afternoon."

Sure enough, everyone in their party had arrived, and they were trading ideas on what they wanted to do for the next few hours.

"I vote for some shopping," Nora Winslow stated, reaching for her third helping of corn bread. "But not until I finish every bit of this delicious confection. I don't have to watch my weight," she announced complacently. "Bob likes me just the way I am. All the more to love, he says."

Ed Mason snorted his impatience. "I'm going to find a good movie, or... Say, Dak, is there a bar around here where a guy can get a decent drink and meet some of the locals, or is the place full of cutesy ice-cream parlors?"

Dak masked his disgust with a shrug. If the guy wanted to meet locals, there were plenty of places to find them outside of bars. From what Dak had seen of Mason so far, it was more likely the guy wanted to pick up a woman. If he headed for a bar, it was anyone's guess when they would see him again.

"Better stick around. You're going to want a ride back to the inn. We'll be going back in a couple of hours."

Mason's restless gaze settled on Mary Lowe while he downed his beer. Dak could see the wheels in Mason's head turning, his eyes light up as he decided on his prey. Poor Mary. Richard's third wife was more than a generation younger than her middle-aged husband and his peers had always appeared lost whenever he'd met her at a Toyland gathering. What she'd seen in Lowe was beyond his understanding, but they'd been married for three years. Maybe she'd needed a father figure, Dak decided. That she was ripe for the picking was obvious. And Ed Mason, with his younger, flattering attention was gearing up for the harvest.

"Katie and I are going down the street to the Aames Art Gallery to view the latest in local art," Dak told Mary. "Care to accompany us?"

"How about coming with me, Mary?" Mason interrupted. "It would be a shame to hide such a lovely young thing as you in an art gallery. There are lots more interesting things we can do together.''

''Oh no,'' Nora broke in. ''We're going shopping and we need Mary's advice, don't we, Molly? Elaine?''

Dak saw that the older woman understood the situation and intended to keep Mary out of harm's way.

''Okay, count me out,'' Mason said crossly. ''I'll catch up with you in a couple of hours.'' He rose, dropped a ten-dollar bill on the table. ''Tell the waitress to keep the change,'' he remarked disdainfully as he left. ''Good thing Cynthia likes to play golf.''

''We're going to drive down to the beach,'' Ellen Fraser announced, her arm in Steve's. ''I'm going to show Steve the mission, and a few other things,'' she added with a giggle.

Dak nodded. Steve shrugged as if to say, what's a guy to do? ''Go on. But don't forget to return for the ladies. Katie and I will see you later.'' Dak was more than satisfied with the way things had turned out. The two people he least wanted around Katie were out of his hair. He took her arm and led her out of the restaurant.

''Most of the artwork comes from local residents,'' Dak explained as he and Katie walked to the gallery. ''Carmel started out as an artists' colony, but it's so famous now everyone wants to visit.''

''It is lovely, isn't it?'' she remarked as they made their way along the picturesque thoroughfare. ''Unfortunately, I'm not into art.''

''But you are creative.'' He cast a sidelong glance at her. ''Very creative.''

''Hardly.'' She stopped to consider the comment. ''No, I don't think so.''

"Take it from me, you are. Creativity takes many forms. Here's the art gallery. You never know what you might find."

He was right, and what she found was a little too much to share her reaction with him. Nude sculptures, large and small, filled the area. A modernistic version of Rodin's *The Kiss* held a place of honor, and in another prominent spot...

"Oh my goodness!" Katie turned her head away. "I'm going outside for a breath of fresh air," she stammered, and hurried out the door. Behind her, she heard Dak exchange a few words with a clerk before he followed her.

"Too much for you?"

"No. I guess I'm just not into modernistic art," she answered as she walked quickly down the street and made for the sanctuary of a toy store. "This is more my style."

In the store, she held up a lifelike doll that said "Mama" when its tummy was squeezed, a pair of boy dolls dressed as Tom Sawyer and Huckleberry Finn and a toy poodle.

"Look, Dak," she said as she turned them over. "Toyland products."

"Interesting, but these are more my style," he answered, going over to a display of futuristic toy cars. "We made these last year and they're still popular, but not enough. Next year we have to make it big."

Katie browsed through the selection of toys, finally picking up some paints and crayons for her nephew. Her last choice was a little girl's jewelry box with an exotic dancer on the lid. She searched for Dak, found him in the next aisle watching toy trains chugging along miniature tracks.

The soft smile on his face brought a smile to her own. He might be a super sleuth, but he looked like a little boy.

When he noticed her observing him, he returned her smile. "I collect toy trains. What's your weakness?"

"All kinds of toys."

"Me, too."

"Is that why you chose to work for Toyland?" Katie inquired.

"You found me out! I guess you're right," he added, glancing at his watch and gathering up several small cars, a train station and a crossroads signal. "I can use these for my collection. I guess I'm a kid who never grew up. What are you buying?"

"Just a few things for my nephew the artist, and a jewelry box for my niece."

"Can she actually dance?" he asked, touching the tiny figure on the lid.

In reply, Katie wound up the music box. She saw him glance at his watch. She should have known. The Mickey Mouse watch he wore was a dead giveaway. He had a boyish side to him that he hadn't shown until she'd seen it at the beach and now in the toy store. In private life he was human after all. Too flesh and blood for her own good.

Dak studied her as she walked ahead of him back to the car. His body responded to her graceful movements, the sway of her hips. There was something about the way she walked that made him want to place his hands on her waist, feel the vibration of her body, enjoy the sensuous aura that seemed to surround her. Maybe it wasn't intentional, but with each step she took it was as if she moved in time to exotic music. Graceful, sensuous, beckoning. In her own fashion,

Katie was a born dancer, a Mata Hari spinning a web calculated to entrap, seduce. And damn, she sure had ensnared him.

Although she'd claimed to have two left feet when they'd danced last night, the personnel file he'd studied with more than casual interest had indicated otherwise. His investigation had revealed something very interesting. Yes, indeed. Katie had a knack for dancing...with tinkling bells, seven veils and sheer, bejeweled costumes that revealed more than they concealed. In her undergraduate days, Katie O'Connor had been a belly dancer.

Chapter Six

Dak had plenty to think about as he drove back to the inn—all of it having to do with the intriguing woman at his side. It should have been obvious from the first moment he'd laid eyes on her that Katie had a dancer's training. Those legs were a dancer's trademark; they should have been a dead giveaway. Why hadn't he realized it before? he mused.

The trouble was, everything about her got in the way of his objective thinking. Those long legs, the rounded calves, the slender ankles, the high-arched foot.

But in spite of those legs and the effect they had on him, he was having a hard time forgiving her for trying to take over the project. Sure she was innovative, but she was also ambitious and headstrong in a business that called for logical and conservative thinking like his own. It would be okay if all he admired was her strength of purpose and the thorough way she handled her job. But there was more to it than that. He was in charge of site planning and security at Toyland, after all, and she should have consulted him. He would never have agreed to a honeymoon inn and an agenda that called for all kinds of secret shenanigans.

And yes, they could have made a good team. Except that she would undoubtedly have been a pain in the neck. He knew from experience that her kind never gave up.

So why had Neil Gibson handed over the planning of the conference, tied with ribbons, to her? And why had she been surprised when Dak had taken exception to it? Could it have been that Neil had been amused by Katie's proposal in a weakened moment? If so, he'd handed Dak a barrel of trouble. And there was McDuff. He had a hunch that this person was somehow tied into that story. He intended to find the answers to those questions. All he had to do was keep a close watch on her.

Under the circumstances, it wasn't going to be easy to get on a friendlier footing with Katie, but he had to try. Not only because he suspected she was hiding something, but because she drew him like a bear to a honeycomb.

What else about her had he missed?

"I think I'd just like to take a long, hot tub bath and have my dinner in the room tonight, instead of eating with the others," Katie announced as they reached the inn as dusk was falling. "The long drive and a sleepless night on the couch are catching up with me." She cast Dak a reproachful look. "But don't let that stop you from eating out."

"Oh no, you don't. You can't blame me for the couch. If you hadn't gone to meet your other husband, you'd have had the bed to yourself. As it was, I just couldn't see it going to waste." He took her packages and helped her out of the car. "As for having dinner alone, what would everyone think if I showed up without my bride? You ought to know it might blow our cover. Tell you what, I'll order up room service for both of us."

"Suit yourself," she answered nonchalantly as she made her way to the entrance of the inn. "As for me, I intend to take a long, hot bath."

A long, hot bath. Lost in the picture of her in the spacious tub, Dak slowed his footsteps. Maybe suite 105 was too dangerous a playground for him just yet.

Loaded with packages, he trailed behind her through the foyer. He could see Steve and Ellen, heads together, at the adjoining bar. Steve looked up and waved to him as he passed. What kind of a guy would abandon Katie so easily? Dak wondered darkly. Surely not a boyfriend. So who was he? And what were he and Ellen plotting after they had supposedly just met? He made up his mind to find out a lot more about Steve Dana, and soon.

Mrs. Fraser motioned him to come to the small reception desk where she was sorting mail. "I need to apologize for what I'm about to say, Dak, but I'm more than a little concerned with Mr. Dana's presence here. I've just found out that when he arrived with Katie, he told our bellhop, Herb, that they were married. And even though he knows you and Katie are registered as man and wife, Herb has already mentioned to the housekeeper and several of the maids that Steve and Katie are married!" She clasped her hands against her chest and went on to tell him about finding Katie outside Dana's quarters last night. "I don't know what to think! I fear for the inn's reputation, and your own."

"Steve's a great one for jokes, Mrs. F. Don't give it another thought." Dak shifted the packages in his arms and caught one as it was about to fall. He smiled

with what he hoped was reassurance. "I'll take care of
Herb and I'll tell Steve to knock off the humor."

"And then, don't think I'm a busybody, but there's
my Ellen's reputation to think of!"

"Of course. I'll talk to Steve about that, too," he
called over his shoulder as he backed away. From what
he'd seen, Ellen Fraser knew how to take care of herself. "At any rate," he added, "we'll all be gone in a
few days."

Water was running into the bathtub as he came into
the suite. He heard a faint splash as something
dropped into the hot water. Bath oil? he wondered as
a faint scent of honeysuckle drew him closer to the
bathroom door. Katie sure didn't need the help of oil,
he thought as he inhaled deeply. Her own wonderful
scent had already gotten to him.

Aided by the faint glow of the bathroom lights, he
could see her reflection in the mirror on the half-open
bathroom door. She was moving slowly, discarding
her sweater, inch by inch—almost, it seemed to him,
thread by thread. Then she had removed the crocheted sweater, drawn her blouse over her head, then
shimmied out of her slacks. She was left with only bikinis and a matching bra of pastel pink satin edged in
lace, which cupped her breasts and framed her soft
glowing skin. He tried to breathe. Couldn't.

He edged forward and saw a white hand, slender,
elegant fingers beckoning. Beckoning? To whom?
Him? No, she couldn't be. Then what the devil *was* she
doing?

He started to turn away, as any gentleman would
have, when her actions became even more intriguing.
Watching herself in the mirrored wall, Katie wrapped
her right hand around her left wrist and stretched four

times. Then she repeated the same movement with her left hand and right wrist. Suddenly she dropped forward, her hands on the floor, and bounced...like a rag doll!

Exercises, he thought with an indulgent smile and a shiver of something more than appreciation of the obvious results of her workouts. Katie didn't need to exercise. As far as he was concerned, she was already in damn good shape.

As she moved to some sort of music she alone heard, he watched her bring her left foot forward, point her toe and swing her left hip. She did the same with her right foot and hip. At the same time, she threw her head back, raised her arms in the air and moved her hands in graceful circles. Fascinating, he thought through quick, short breaths. But he wasn't looking at her arms all that much. Not when she rotated her hips in a sensuous figure eight and swayed to the silent music.

She was doing a belly dance, no less, Dak decided. Surprised and intrigued by her dancing, he edged closer. He'd seen a few belly dancers in his time, but nothing like this. His mouth turned dry and his body responded in a way that was downright embarrassing! He had to leave before she realized he was there.

He couldn't.

He should.

He didn't want to.

A further undulating movement of her hips held him rapt. Her legs were long, slender, the skin was a warm amber. Her foot arched; her pink toes tensed and relaxed, tensed and relaxed. She rose higher, again arching her feet. His gaze moved up her calves. His hands ached to stroke her silken thighs, the satin strap of her bikinis, the womanly hips. Dak's heartbeat accelerated to the music. Music? Good Lord, he was hearing music! Now he knew he was in trouble!

He closed his eyes and backed away from the door. Katie had been right. He had all the instincts of a voyeur. And the fatal weakness of a man.

There was the sound of a splash when Katie got into the sunken tub. He didn't have to watch to know what she did next, to be able to visualize what she looked like when she used the bath sponge to rinse off her neck, her arms, her breasts. Or when she raised her legs one by one and slowly, sensuously, ran the sponge down over her skin. No, sir. In his body and mind he was beside her every step of the way.

Where was the ice machine when a man needed a very long, very cold drink?

He moved quickly to the minibar in the living room, considered a stiff drink, then discarded the idea. He had to be alert and responsible in order to resist temptation for the rest of the evening. And after seeing Katie doing her striptease it wasn't going to be easy. He had to keep his wits about him so he could keep an eye on her in case she decided to visit her other "husband" later that night. Dana had caused enough problems with his loose tongue, without Katie being caught sneaking in and out of his cottage. His stomach reminded him he was hungry. Low-cal chili hadn't been enough.

"Room service? I'd like dinner for two sent to suite 105. What's on the menu tonight? Great, hang on a minute."

He carried the phone to the bedroom door. "Katie? How about shrimp in lobster sauce on a bed of angel-hair pasta and all the trimmings for dinner?"

"Broiled shrimp, rice and a salad, please," she called back. "And lemon sorbet, if they have it."

Dak repeated her order into the telephone. "Make it for two, please." Visions of hunger pains in the night from such a light meal floated in front of him. What the hell. As long as it wasn't chocolate, Katie couldn't possibly object to seeing his favorite pie on the table. He intended to have a decent dessert. "And by the way, if you have lemon pie on the menu, include a man-size portion, too. In an hour. Thanks."

"Need to have me wash your back?" he yelled through the bedroom doors.

Wearing a short terry-cloth robe, a towel wrapped around her wet hair and smelling like fresh-picked honeysuckle blossoms, Katie appeared in the doorway. "You wish."

"Guilty as charged." His eyes traveled over her carefully, starting with the damp auburn tendrils peeking out from under the towel, down her shapely legs to her pink toes, and he sighed over what was hidden in between. "Isn't that what husbands do?"

"*If* you were my husband, which you're not," she retorted firmly as she disappeared into the bedroom. "I'll be out in a jiffy. When's dinner coming? I'm starved."

It was going to be a long evening, Dak thought as he headed for the small bar. He was starved, too, but it wasn't for broiled shrimp, rice and a salad.

"SOME LEMON PIE?"

Katie swallowed the last of the lemon sorbet and considered the giant-size slice of pie Dak was offering her. If he only knew; lemon-flavored food was an-other weakness of hers. But while she'd been able to find a Chocoholics Anonymous chapter, she'd never been able to locate a lemon anything. Maybe because lemons were full of vitamin C, she thought virtuously, and actually healthy. A bite or two of the pie seemed an okay thing to do. She picked up a clean spoon. "Just a bite."

She noticed Dak observing her with avid interest as she dug her spoon into the corner of the lemon meringue pie. She held it to her lips, tasted and chewed with solemn concentration.

"Great!" When she remembered the way he'd eaten the chocolate cupcake in her office, deliberately, sensuously, the devil took ahold of her. She duplicated his actions with another bite and watched Dak's reaction as she slowly licked the last of the meringue from her lips. A flush rose over his face before he abruptly turned away. Good, she thought; that ought to teach him not to try to seduce her with food or anything else.

Face the facts, Katie O'Connor, she thought as she noted his reaction to her studied reprisal; where Dak Smith was concerned, she could be seduced. Sexy Smith, she decided to call him. And, oh yes, he was very alluring. She closed her eyes and thought of the way his tongue would duel with hers if she let him kiss her, the way his solid arms would feel holding her tightly against him and the way his fingers would feel sliding—

Her eyes popped open. One more sensual thought and she would find herself in his arms.

Dak waited until Katie laid down her spoon. Dinner was finished, and so was he if he didn't get to the next order of business in a hurry. "And now for the big decision."

"And that is?" Katie inquired as she casually repaired her lipstick and adjusted the lounging pajamas she was wearing.

"Who gets to sleep in the bed."

"You mean you're actually willing to have me sleep on the couch while you take the bed? I can't believe you. What happened to chivalry?"

"Dead with King Arthur." Dak sighed as he joined her and cautiously eyed the couch as if its presence offended him. "Trying to sleep on that couch was pure torture. On the other hand," he said as his gaze swept over her, "you're small enough to fit in it comfortably." And petite enough to fit into his arms, he thought. "Any ideas how we can settle this?"

Katie swung around. She was in no mood for his tricks. "Sleeping on the couch wasn't a picnic for me, either. But, if you're serious about taking the bed, I'll toss you for it."

Dak looked over at the stack of wrapped packages resting in a chair. "I've got a better idea. I'll play you for it."

"Play me for it?" Her eyes narrowed. "What kind of play did you have in mind?"

"Now, now. You continue to surprise me with the way your liberated mind works," Dak scolded. "Give me some credit for being a gentleman."

"If you were a gentleman, you'd sleep on the couch."

"I'm a gentleman, all right, but I draw the line at narrow couches. Come now, don't tell me you're afraid to settle this by playing a game with me?"

"Okay. If it's a game you want, a game is what you'll get." Katie marched over to the packages. "Choose your weapon."

"Scrabble?" he asked, remembering the number of games she'd added to her purchases that afternoon in Carmel. It wasn't what he wanted to play, but he was pretty sure she wasn't in the mood for what he had in mind.

"It takes too long. I'm tired and I want to go to bed."

Dak considered his wily opponent. Her restless eyes belied her poker face. He could tell she wanted something more than the bed and he was keeping her from getting to it. He wanted something, too. But he also wanted more than just the bed. He still wanted her in it. Warm and willing.

He wanted to awaken in the morning after a night of loving to find her there beside him. He wanted to drown himself in her flashing green eyes, to hold her close and savor the scent of her that was uniquely hers. He wanted her to do a belly dance just for him. This time to real music, so he could properly get in the mood to appreciate the performance. On the other hand, he decided as his body responded to the thought, maybe not. Flesh and blood could stand just so much.

A quick glance at his watch told him it was barely nine o'clock. Even as he considered what game he could play to beat her to bed, he knew that, as sure as his name was Dakota Smith, Katie was planning on pretending to go to sleep early—and to sneak out of the suite during the night and go to Steve Dana's cottage. She had a surprise coming. He didn't intend to fall asleep no matter who won. Wherever she would go, he intended to follow. And find out what she was up to.

"Well, you bought enough games to be able to agree on something." He rummaged through the packages. "What's in this one?"

"A deck of dinosaur playing cards. I bought it for my nephew, Michael."

"It'll do. Know any card games?"

"A perfect one—War," she answered with confidence. "I've played it with Michael hundreds of times. I should warn you I usually win. Let's see if you're any better at it than he is." Katie cleared off the coffee table and opened the package of cards with a flourish. "Deal."

Dak knew what War was all about, but not the way she obviously intended to play it. To her, it was going to be more than a game. It was going to be a fight to the finish. Well, he could handle that. He shuffled the deck and, brushing the warm hand that reached for the cards, dealt half the deck facedown to Katie. He wasn't going to be able to play, he thought with a frown as her hand covered his, not if she was going to keep touching him. "Hands off until I'm ready."

"Ready? This *is* only a card game, isn't it?" Katie asked as she snatched her hand away.

"Sure, but the stakes are pretty high," Dak said seriously as he dealt the other half of the deck facedown to himself. He had to try hard to concentrate when her fresh scent of bath oil got in the way of his thinking. "You first."

She turned over the first card, slapped it on the table. It was a jack. "Beat that!" she said, her voice dripping with satisfaction. "I dare you."

He won with a queen.

She turned over a ten.

He turned over a king and won again.

Her next card was a seven. She eyed Dak's next card, also a seven, with hope. She still had a chance to win. "War!" she declared as she put three more cards on the table facedown. Her fourth card was another king. "My luck changed," she crowed. "I knew it would."

Dak dealt out his three cards facedown. His fourth card was an ace. "Looks as if I've won again," he commented lazily in answer to her muted groan.

The game continued until he had won all of her cards. Katie ground her teeth in frustration. She couldn't stand the idea of sleeping on the couch, even for an hour. Or giving him the satisfaction of sleeping in the bed. "Two games out of three?"

"Sure," Dak agreed, glancing at his watch. "The night is young. Unless you're planning an early get-away?"

"Yeah. Getaway into that big bed and sleep," she snapped. "Pay attention to the game."

Two games later, Dak was still the winner. Katie stood and regally announced, "I'll change in the bathroom and *then* you can have the bed."

Dak swept her a courtly bow. "Of course. Ladies first." He whistled while he packed the cards and set the serving cart with its empty dishes outside the door. He was browsing through the complimentary videos when she came back into the room wearing her navy blue sweats.

"Planning on prowling the grounds again tonight?" he asked, "or is that the latest in sleeping attire?"

"They're comfortable, that's all. Besides, what do you think I'd wear, under the circumstances? A negligee from Victoria's Secret?" A pillow under one arm and a blanket under the other, she glanced scornfully at Dak and headed for the couch. "Turn out the lights when you leave."

Dak retreated behind the bedroom doors. He chuckled to himself as he washed loudly enough for her to hear and then made himself comfortable on the bed. He piled the pillows behind him and settled down to outwait Katie. He'd give her an hour before she thought it was safe to leave the suite.

Exactly an hour later by his watch he heard the door to the suite close softly behind her. Predictable Katie, bless her, was on her way to visit her other "husband." Just what she was trying to accomplish was beyond him. Unless... He sat up with a start and mentally finished his own sentence. Unless she didn't trust herself around him.

The idea was fascinating and strangely flattering. Never one to pursue a woman who wasn't interested, and certainly not a strong-minded one who reminded him of his ex, he was still very much aware of the attraction Katie held for him. Suspect or not. Just the idea that she might feel the same way about him set his thoughts afire.

By the time she had taken a roundabout route to the guest cottage in an effort to avoid the lit path, the weather had taken a turn for the worse. A faint new moon, obscured by fog drifting up from the ocean, lent its eerie presence. A dog howled in the distance. Another one barked its answer. Soon a trio of dogs were howling their distress. Trees bowed under the increasing wind, their branches reaching out to clutch her as she made her way through the grounds. There was a flash of lightning and a loud clap of thunder. Heavy raindrops fell in sheets. Then there was a deep silence, broken only by the sound of the rain and the surf as it pounded against the rocks below the cliffs.

The cliffs! Katie thought with a shudder. Beautiful in the sunlight, dangerous at night. She had to be careful where she walked or she could drop off into the ocean! She slowed her pace and carefully continued her way through the grounds.

Ahead, she could see the dim outline of a building. Her heart pounding at the Halloween-like darkness, she hurried toward safety. There was another flash of lightning followed by a clap of thunder. The trees shook under a renewed strong gust of wind that moaned its way around her. Katie shivered. Maybe this hadn't been such a good idea. She became certain of it when the grounds suddenly were plunged into darkness.

She froze, then twirled around at the sharp sound of a branch being whipped from a tree. Disoriented, she lost her sense of direction. Where there had been a dim outline of a building, now she could see only black. Pitch-black darkness everywhere. Buffeted by the winds, she sought to find some familiar landmark. She wrapped her arms around herself and wished she hadn't been foolish enough to leave the safety of the suite.

Suddenly she spotted the dim glow of a flashlight. "Over here, please!" she called, "I could use some help in getting back to the inn."

"It's me, Katie." Flashlight in hand, Steve called to her as he fought his way through strong gusts of wind to her side. "I was hoping to catch you before you came this far. The storm's caused a power outage. You'd be better off in the main building."

"I know. Thank goodness you're here." She peered through the blackness. "I don't even know where I am. I was afraid I was going to fall off a cliff!"

"Hold on to me and I'll take you as far as the main building. I was headed there before the power failed."

"You were supposed to wait for me at the cottage!"

"I left the door open in case I didn't connect with you, but I don't think you'd be very happy there by yourself." By the light of his flashlight, Steve surveyed her shivering form thoughtfully. "You know, I don't understand why you want to stay in the cottage with me at night, anyway. Or why you hired me to play your husband, when you have Dak. Mind telling me what's going on?"

"Not now, for Pete's sake. I'll tell you later," Katie said worriedly. "Look over there. I can see the building. Thank goodness they painted it pink. You can go on to wherever you were going. I'll be all right now." Impulsively she kissed his cheek. "Thanks for coming to find me."

"I'd better come with you until you're safely inside. No, really," he said as she protested. "I'd feel a lot better knowing you were out of this. Besides, I'm expected. Someone will probably come to meet me in a minute."

"Ellen?"

"Yeah. I didn't think you'd mind."

"No." Katie shivered as the cold rain pounded down. They started toward the faint outline of the main building ahead.

Suddenly she spotted Dak coming down the path with a flashlight of his own. "What are you doing out here?" she called out angrily. "Following me?"

"Someone needs to save you from yourself." Dak frowned as he came up to them and eyed Steve. "Only a nitwit would let Katie go out into a storm like this. Couldn't you have persuaded her to stay inside with me tonight?"

Steve threw up his hands. "So help me, this wasn't my idea!"

"Everything would have been fine if there hadn't been a power failure," Katie rejoined. "And if you hadn't set out to spy on me."

"What were the two of you doing out here, anyway?" he demanded. "Don't you have enough sense to come in out of the rain?"

"What Steve and I do is none of your business."

Steve shrugged. "A gentleman never tells on a lady."

Katie groaned. "Don't be ridiculous, Steve. You make it sound as if there's more to it than there is." She turned to Dak. "I just needed some fresh air. I didn't think a storm and a blackout would occur."

"Fresh air! Come on, do I look that stupid?" Dak snorted. "There's more to this than a sudden yen for fresh air, but now's not the time to discuss it."

In spite of her protests, Dak grabbed her by the arm and started back to the inn. He left Steve to follow them. "Just hold on to me and keep your head down. All sorts of things are flying around."

Fighting the gusts of wind and the driving rain, they made their way back to the inn.

The halls were crowded with guests milling around in an assortment of nightclothes. Mrs. Fraser and Herb, busily assuring everyone that the lights would come on soon, were passing out flashlights. Nora Winslow spotted the trio and came hurrying over.

"What on earth are you all doing outside on a night like this?" she asked as she eyed the dripping trio. "And who is this man?"

Herb laughed. "They're her two husbands."

"Her two husbands?" She peered at Steve Dana. "I thought Dak was her husband."

"It depends on who's doing the introductions," Herb replied with a laugh.

"Herbert! Tend to your own business," Mrs. Fraser absentmindedly admonished as she waited to hear Katie's answer.

"Wouldn't mind sticking around to hear their story." Herb leered at Katie before continuing to distribute flashlights.

"Katie!" Nora said, curiosity getting the better of her. "What did Herb mean when he said you had two husbands?"

Katie, cringing on the inside, saw a small group of onlookers, lit flashlights in hand, avidly listening for her answer. Beside her, Dak gazed silently at her under raised eyebrows. She could see that Steve wasn't going to be any help, either. Two husbands were two too many, but she was darned if she knew how to explain it. Swallowing her pride, she cast an appealing look at Dak.

"It was just a misguided joke, Nora." Dak put his arm around Katie. "Obviously it hasn't gone over very well. Steve here is Katie's brother."

Ellen Fraser joined the group. "Steve, come on over to my room and get out of your wet things."

Nora Winslow appeared more astonished than ever. "Well, I never! What is this world coming to?"

"We'll see you in the morning, Nora. I'm sure we'll all be in a better mood to enjoy the joke." Dak urged

Katie down the hall. "Better leave before you get into deeper water," he muttered. "Especially since you don't seem to know how to swim."

This time, Katie was more than happy to follow him. She fell into the suite. "I've never in my life been so grateful to be back indoors," she said as she tried the light switch. "There's no power in here, either."

Dak peeled off his windbreaker and his wet shirt. "I could use a hot shower, but you go first. Take your flashlight with you. As soon as I get out of these soaking shoes I'll find you a robe."

In the glare of the flashlight, Katie could see water glistening on Dak's chest. Under her fascinated gaze, a few drops slid down his skin and made their way to his belted waist. As he bent over to take off his rain-soaked shoes, arm and shoulder muscles rippled invitingly. Impulsively she reached out to touch his solid strength, only to pull back when he straightened.

He smiled as he caught her interested gaze riveted on his chest. "See something that interests you?" he asked. He grinned when she tossed her head and made for the bedroom.

Damn, she'd almost been caught in the act of making a fool of herself!

She left the flashlight shining on a bench while she took a quick, hot shower. She could have stayed under the hot needlelike stream forever, but she knew Dak was cold and wet, too. He tossed a robe around the door. She drew it around her and, by the light of the flashlight, came back into the bedroom.

"My turn," he said. "Why don't you get into bed and stay warm?"

The covers had been thrown aside. Down the middle of the bed, Dak had strung huge down pillows neatly dividing the king-size bed into two.

"Choose your side and hop in," he called from the bathroom. "I'll be out in a minute. You'll feel much better as soon as you've dried off and had a good night's sleep."

Katie eyed the bed. Bundling, a 1990s version, was back.

"I don't want to appear ungrateful, but I'm not sure this is the wisest thing to do," Katie said carefully when he came into the bedroom dressed in a matching robe.

"No? Would you rather take the couch?"

A loud clap of thunder, followed by a fierce gust of wind, shook the building. Rain pounded with renewed fury against the windows. It was too much for her. "I'll take the far side," she announced as she hurried around the bed. "After I find a nightgown."

"I didn't know you had any," Dak answered as he toweled his hair. "All you've worn for the past two nights were those confounded sweats."

"Never mind, I'll sleep in the robe," Katie muttered as there was crack of lightning, followed by another clap of thunder. She fell into bed and covered herself with the down cover. Dak turned off the flashlight. A soft whoosh of terry cloth and a movement of the covers told her he had undressed before climbing onto his side of the bed.

Good Lord, why hadn't she realized he might take off his robe before getting into bed? And that he might be in the habit of sleeping nude. Nude! She could envision his bare body. Tall, lean of waist, broad of shoulders. And well muscled. She knew that from seeing him after he'd taken off his dripping shirt.

His presence only inches away awakened feelings in Katie she'd never expected and wasn't sure she was ready for. No matter how much he got to her. Certainly feelings she didn't need now that they were in the same bed together. And certainly not when she was so aware of his sheer masculinity. She inched farther away from the fragile pillow barrier. Rather than feeling secure in the knowledge that they were separated by a barricade of pillows, she knew her awakened hormones were sending her senses spinning.

Chapter Seven

Was it the sound of rain that had awakened her?

Katie was dimly aware of embracing the pillow that separated her side of the bed from Dak's. Strange, she thought sleepily, the pillow was so warm, so alive, almost as if it had a life of its own. She burrowed into its softness and started to drift back to sleep.

When the pillow stirred under her arms, she opened her eyes. Good heavens, she thought in dismay, it wasn't a pillow she was embracing. It was Dak!

She started to pull away, before she realized he'd thrown his arm around her in his sleep. One very warm, muscled thigh and long leg held her captive. Pinned to his chest, she felt a rising tide of desire sweep through her. She was afraid to move, scared she might awaken him. Terrified to see the look in his eyes when he discovered her in his arms. She lay there quietly, hoping he would turn over in his sleep and let her go before he awakened, yet wanting to stay this way forever. Praying for an early dawn and the chance to slide out of the bed, she listened to the storm beating against the windows.

The rain was what had made her decide to throw good sense out the window and share the bed. She'd been afraid of lightning and thunder ever since she'd been a small child. Her brothers had teased her, until she'd learned to hide her fears, but they were still with her. With Dak so understanding, the storm had been a legitimate excuse for her to sleep beside him, to feel safe. Or had it been something more?

His fresh, musky scent intoxicated her. She could feel the steady beat of his heart, the warmth of his taut skin against her own. The strong and sure muscular arm that held her pinned to him. Almost as if he were afraid to let her go. His chest, pressed against her own, rose and fell to measured breathing. She pictured his reaction if he should awake and find her caught in his embrace. After the way she'd insisted on separate sleeping arrangements, would he understand it was an accident? That in her sleep she'd only been seeking refuge from the storm?

Katie knew what men thought of a woman who teased and didn't deliver. She didn't want him to think she was one those. On the other hand, she didn't know just what she wanted, she realized as she tried to edge away from him. When she stirred uneasily, he murmured her name, his arm tightened and held her prisoner.

Even as she waited for a chance to slip out of bed, she realized she didn't want to move just yet. In spite of their differences, she was deeply aware she'd been attracted to Dak for days; had wondered how his arms would feel around her, how it would feel to be kissed by him as though he really meant it.

It didn't matter, she thought with soft sigh. Just being in his arms was wonderfully satisfying. A smile tugged at her lips and she nestled closer into the enveloping heat of his body.

A break in his steady breathing told her he was awake. She cautiously turned her head, to find those disturbing hazel eyes watching her. Her gaze lingered on his features. The high arch of his brows, the long dark lashes that no man should have been given. The curved line of lips meant for lingering kisses. In his intent gaze and quirked eyebrow, there was a silent question.

She ran her tongue over her suddenly dry lips, heard the drumming of her quickened heartbeat. Her eyes locked with his; she couldn't move or speak, not when her fantasy was about to come true.

Without saying a word, his hand stroked her waist where the robe had fallen open, slid up her body and lightly cupped her breasts. His warm hand left a trail of fire, igniting her desire along the way. That age-old man-woman question was in his eyes. For a moment, she hesitated. How could she face him later? What would he think of her? But did it matter, after all? She was where she wanted to be. She let herself be caught by the web of desire he seemed to have woven around her.

His body was on fire as he pulled her closer to him, bare skin to bare skin. Heat to heat. Her body throbbed in response as he pulled her up to face him. His first kiss was a soft welcome. Their mouths, their lips, their tongues touched. Tentatively at first, then fiercely driven by desire.

"Is this what you want? If not, let's quit now before I can't stop," he whispered as he slowly rubbed his hand down the curve of her hip to where her desire flamed. He kissed her breasts until the nipples hardened. Nipped gently until she pressed against his hand, wanting more. When he obliged, she clung to him. Nothing mattered but these moments.

She knew he wanted her, but the pride that shone from his eyes told her he would go no further than she wanted him to. Hesitating, she ran her hands across his face, kissed him with all the pent-up desire in her and answered, "Yes, oh yes!"

This was a new Dak, her heart told her, as she brushed his dark hair from his forehead and answered his questioning smile with a reassuring one of her own. Somehow she sensed she was seeing a side of him he seldom shared with anyone else. Gone was his need for dominance, his need to be strong. He was asking instead of telling. Tender instead of brusque. Her heart responded to him. She raised her lips to him again.

As he continued to run his hand across her heated skin and feathered her face with kisses, she felt light-headed with desire. He must have felt it, too. His hazel eyes softened, a tender smile curved at the corner of his lips. He leaned forward and kissed her in the hollow between her breasts.

"Katie, sweet Katie" she heard him murmur, before he eased her back against the pillows and kissed her throat, her cheeks, her lips. All coherent thought flew out of her mind as he pressed against her and took her head between his hands.

Her mouth moved under his, tasted him as he was devouring her. She licked his skin, tasted the salty sweat of him. Bared her neck for him to kiss. A sweet languor spread over her as his lips moved along her nape to touch her ear with the tip of his tongue and linger there. To probe, to taste.

"Take off your robe, Katie," he whispered. Under his soft urging, she pulled it off, giving herself up to the flame that enveloped her. All the nonsense that had gone between them before this moment no longer mattered. Her need for him had become as great as his seemed to be for her. When his hands stroked her skin as if he were playing a fine instrument, she willingly surrendered her body for him to take. When his knee parted her legs, she rose to meet him, to make him part of her inner core. Her legs tightened around him, urging him deeper. She matched him, movement for movement. She needed more of him, everything he could give.

As if he knew what she wanted, needed, he thrust against her until her movements instinctively matched his. Sigh for sigh, meeting thrust with her own seeking, searching body, she clasped him closer still. Murmuring his name, her needs, she felt him accelerate his movements.

He carried her to the stars, let her linger there for a moment while he gazed down at her. "Dak?" she cried, teetering on the edge of something powerful. With a final, urgent thrust, he answered her, pushing her over into the heavens that seemed to surround her.

Katie dimly heard the thunder of his heart, his strained, whispered words of passion. In the darkness, stars exploded behind her eyes, breaking into hundreds of tiny crystals that drifted over her from a star-lit sky. She floated on a cloud of sensual pleasure as she felt his release. The feeling of completion was so great she clung to him long after he collapsed at her side.

She'd never remembered feeling so wonderful, so complete. Why had she never known this aching love-

liness was waiting for her? Only with Dak, her mind
and body told her. She pressed even closer to him,
kissed him hungrily, yearning for more of the taste and
feel of him. She didn't want the moment to end.

The storm beating against the windows echoed the
one sweeping through her, sending her back into a
maelstrom of sensuality. She pushed herself up and lay
across his glistening chest. Kissed his nipples, touched
him as he had her.

"Ah, my Katie. Fire within, and fire without," he
said, stroking her auburn hair.

She felt his desire rise against her again as he tumbled her back onto the bed. A heated tide swept over
her, stealing her breath away, before it pulled her under and tossed her again and again into a whirlpool of
heightened sensations.

SHE AWAKENED to find herself still in Dak's arms, reluctant to move. A faint light shone from the next
room; power had been restored. Still, she was reluctant to move an inch.

She felt the rasp of his unshaven cheek against her
own as he moved restlessly in his sleep. She inhaled the
pure male salty scent of him, the scent of passion that
lingered, smiled when he whispered her name. The
faint smirk that curved at his lips echoed the smile in
her heart.

The digital clock on the table beside the bed told her
it was five in the morning. And from its faint light she
could find her way around the suite, shower and
change. How long had it been since the moment she'd
lost herself in the crush of Dak's body against her
own? How long since the renewed onslaught to her
senses?

She still didn't know how she would feel later in the morning. She told herself she was a woman of the nineties, entitled to sexual freedom. With five brothers watching over her, eyeing every boyfriend as if each were about to ravish her, her life had largely been circumspect. And boring. Not that she hadn't had the opportunity, but she hadn't found a man she had wanted to share herself with for a long time.

Not until Dak.

She'd funneled her thoughts and energies into her career, hoping to someday meet the right man. Was he that man?

Through the window, she could see the first rays of dawn breaking through the morning mist. Could hear the muffled sounds of the surf breaking against the rocks below the inn. She stretched languorously. A wonderful new day, she told herself. A new beginning.

She turned her head to gaze at Dak. A frown creased his forehead as he muttered a few words, too softly for her to hear. Still asleep, he tightened his arms around her. She snuggled closer, lost herself in his warmth, shut her eyes and drifted back to dream.

Later, much later, time stopped again. He was running his unshaven cheek against hers. He was stroking her body, and his hands lingered, soft and warm. She couldn't stop him, didn't want to. She reached to pull his face down to hers, but he held her away from him. He touched her lips with a gentle finger.

"Hush," he said, "let me. I want to make you happy."

"I am," she said, but her words turned into a moan as he ran his lips down her body.

"Let me kiss you," he said as he stroked her, kissed the inside of her thighs, brought her to the brink of ecstasy once again. With a moan, she let herself sink back into the tide that crashed around her.

"ARE YOU OKAY?" Dak awakened her with a trail of feathery kisses down her shoulder.

"Umm," she murmured into his chest. "I'll never be the same." She looked up into his smiling face. "And you?"

"Never better. I just wondered if you have any regrets." He touched the rosy tip of her breast with a questioning forefinger. "After all, if it hadn't been for the storm, we might still be strangers."

"Strangers?"

"Of a sort." He bent to kiss the tip of her nose. "Did you know you look adorable in the mornings?"

"I'm probably a mess," Katie replied, glancing at her watch. "Goodness, I have to make a phone call."

"Now?"

"It's seven-thirty."

"Oh. Your very efficient timetable is the problem, isn't it? Never mind. The gang can take care of themselves for another half hour. Come here." He reached for her.

"Sorry," she said with a sigh. "There's something I have to do. I'll be back."

Through the slatted door, he could hear her using the telephone. Then he heard her mention the name "McDuff." Each morning at seven-thirty she called and used that name. A code name, perhaps?

"Who's McDuff?" he asked casually as she slid back into bed.

"My dog."

"You expect me to believe that you left me to call your dog?"

"Of course not, silly. Why would I call a dog?"

"Exactly." He lay back against the pillows and regarded her under narrowed eyebrows. "Tell me, Katie, just what are you really up to?"

An unwelcome icy wave crept through her as she realized that he wasn't joking. She had told him the truth about McDuff. She *had* been calling the vet to see how her poor little terrier was getting along without her. Was this the same man who had kissed her so tenderly in the night? The man who'd loved her so passionately again and again. A numbness spread over her. Dak hadn't really changed, after all. She closed her eyes at the realization. He was still the same man. The man she'd angered once before when she'd unwittingly trod on his male ego.

He wasn't the man she'd thought she'd discovered during the long night.

"Perhaps I was mistaken," she said sharply as she mentally berated herself for falling into his arms. "I didn't stop to think you didn't trust me. That this might be just another one-night stand for you."

"One-night stand!" He swung out of bed and stood there angrily gazing at her. His lips were tight, his eyes cold. "You sure know how to cut a man down to size, don't you? Here I thought you were willing to be a woman for me. I thought I'd been mistaken about you, or that you'd changed. But of course not. Not Katie," he mocked. "I just never figured you to be one of those women who take great pleasure in trying to emasculate a man."

Tears stinging her eyes, she could only gaze back at him, feeling helpless. Watch the anger that had taken away the man she thought she'd found. She wished she could disappear, that last night had never happened.

"And now that we know where we stand with each other, what were you and Dana doing out there in the storm last night?"

"What did you say?" Deeply hurt, Katie braced herself for his answer.

"I asked what were you and Dana doing out there kissing in the rain last night?" he repeated as he shrugged into his robe.

"You've got a lot of nerve to ask me that!" She covered herself with the sheet and searched under the blankets with her toes for her discarded robe. She felt outraged, betrayed. "And after last night?"

"Come on now," Dak responded. "Considering you can't wait to get out of here, what does last night have to do with the question?"

"It has everything to do with it!" Katie dove under the covers, found and dragged out the robe she'd discarded in the dark. "How can you sleep with someone you mistrust?" she demanded. She struggled to put the robe around her. It was time to end this. "Or don't you care who you make love with?"

When he saw the tears gather in her emerald eyes, Dak had second thoughts. He suddenly realized he'd probably gone too far, too fast. That he should have listened to her explanations, instead of flying off the handle. That his wounded ego had led him to say things he already regretted. He would have given a lot to take back his harsh words. Not to have asked about this McDuff or Dana at a time like this.

The trouble was, he'd been trained to be conscious of security first; everything else came second. And there was still that something about Katie that triggered his sixth sense whenever he was with her.

"Katie, listen to me," he said as he moved toward her. "It's not that I mistrust you. You turned up here with a man you say is your husband, when your employment record shows you're not married. It's enough to make anyone suspicious. Especially when you go off in the middle of the night in a storm with the guy. Come on, be reasonable."

"Reasonable? Now *I'm* the one who's not reasonable?" She glared at him. "Are you for real or were you trained at *Spy* magazine? You wouldn't be suspicious now unless you had a devious mind to begin with," Katie said, finally making it out of the bed. She drew herself up to her full height as she belted the thick white robe. "I'd appreciate it if you'd go into the other room while I shower and dress. We still have a business meeting at eight-thirty. And, for your information, let me tell you something. We *were* strangers when we met, and as far as I'm concerned, we're strangers still! Last night never happened!"

Dak eyed a tousled Katie. Anger spilled from her tearful eyes. Sparkling green eyes that had drawn him from the first. Warm, sensual eyes that had turned as cold as shards of green glass. A pity. He glanced at the other side of the bed. Scenes of their passionate night played across his mind. "Hardly strangers," he commented dryly.

"Strangers," she repeated firmly. "Last night was a big mistake for both of us. Blame it on the storm. It will never happen again. You have my word on it. Now, if you don't mind, I'd like to get dressed. Please leave."

He saw there was no point in arguing with her. He gave her a mock salute, turned on his heel and left. As he thought about last night's storm, the one outside and the one in her arms, he wasn't willing to bet he wouldn't find her in his embrace again.

When it was his turn to dress, she swept past him as if he were invisible and went out to the balcony. She was dressed in a forest green suit, short jacket, pale green camisole and a knee-length skirt. As she turned her back to him, raindrops fell from the overhang and sparkled like diamonds on her silken hair.

Dak paused in the doorway. She made a lovely picture standing against a backdrop of rain-drenched trees. The sun sparkled on the blue-green ocean in the distance. She was beautiful and he wasn't surprised to find that he was beginning to fall in love with her.

How could he have lost what was left of his common sense where she was concerned? He'd only been doing his job when he'd questioned her. But, as it turned out, it sure had been the wrong time and the wrong place. That showed how much he'd learned about women in all of his thirty-one years.

They'd gone beyond a business relationship last night. And, he realized, far beyond a mere physical attraction. She hadn't been just any woman to him, no matter what she thought. It had been Katie he'd desired, the strong-minded, irritating, but intriguing woman. The feisty lady who could be a closet belly dancer and a businesswoman at the same time. She was like a chameleon, changing personalities with the occasion. Each one attracted him in a different way.

At any rate, he'd have to start to make up with her all over again if he intended to keep a trained eye on her and find out what she was up to. But first, he would make it his business to find out if she'd been telling the truth about her daily early-morning telephone conversations with McDuff—her dog?—and just who Steve Dana really was.

Not that he was jealous of Dana, he told himself for the fifteenth time. He rubbed himself dry after a quick shower and dressed. It was his job to account for everyone attached to the conference, and to keep an eye on other guests at the inn at the same time. He wasn't the jealous type, he insisted.

"Ready?" he asked as he buttoned his navy blue blazer over his gray slacks and ran his fingers through his hair. When Katie started to pass him without a glance, he caught her arm.

"Hold up a minute. I have something I want to say." The forlorn look in her eyes was too much for him. "I'd like to apologize for acting like a jerk in there. You didn't deserve what I said."

When she didn't reply, he tried to joke his way through what was probably one of the most embarrassing moments of his life. "Here, take a swing at me. You'll feel better."

Katie shook her head. "You're right. I didn't deserve it."

"Can we start again?"

"I suppose so. To a point. Anyway, the storm's over. Last night won't happen again."

The storm outside or the one in her heart? Katie wondered as she walked to the door. Dak had made such deep inroads into her heart and senses, she felt she'd remember last night for the rest of her life. How could she have fallen in love with a man who didn't love her?

Dak shrugged and followed her out of the suite to the small sitting room where continental breakfast was served.

Somewhere he'd read that at the Tickle Pink Inn breakfast was served with champagne and a rose on the tray, if requested. He should have asked to have the flower sent to the suite while Katie was dressing. Maybe he was mistaken, but just possibly she would have been moved to forgive him his forthright questions if she'd been gifted with the rose. He stored away the in-room option for another morning. If there was going to be another dawn.

It was too early for most of the guests to be up and about, but the meeting attendees were out in force, their spouses with them.

Bob Winslow, dressed in fishing gear, complete with a cap covered with fishing lures, was urging everyone to finish breakfast so the men could go fishing.

Cynthia Mason, easel and paints at the ready, was munching on a croissant. Her husband, Ed, coffee in hand, lounged against the patio door, eyeing Mary Lowe. The other women whispered at a corner table.

"I'll take the conference room this morning and get everyone started," Katie announced in a cool aside to Dak. "See if you can find something for the others to do today. Maybe Ellen would be willing to take them on a ride. Steve can go along to help, if you don't want to. I'll join you as quickly as I can."

At Katie's exit, as if at a signal, the fishing party said their goodbyes, gathered their belongings and trailed out of the room. "We're going up to Moss Landing," Bob Winslow announced. "Wish us luck. We'll see you ladies later."

Cynthia Mason gathered her paints and easel. "I'm going out to the edge of the cliff and paint the coast-line. The early-morning mist as it drifts over the ocean waves crashing against the rocks is a perfect subject for a landscape."

Nora Winslow snorted. "Fine second honeymoon this is turning out to be. I never see that man of mine except at night. I'm beginning to think I might as well not be along, for all he cares. It's a good thing Katie remembers we're still alive and plans things for us to do."

Dak was amused and impressed to see how well Katie had organized the day's activities. She was damn good at dreaming up the camouflage for the real activities of the toy planners. He had to give her an A for her efforts and an A plus for her imagination.

He'd started over to talk to Mason, when Dana wandered into the room. "Got a minute?" Dak called. Steve turned back to meet him. "I'd like to talk to you."

"Sure." Steve looked surprised and more than a little wary as he glanced first around the room and then back to Dak. "But I've only got a minute. I have to meet someone."

"Yeah, I know. Ellen Fraser. That's another piece of the puzzle that doesn't make any sense." Dak studied him. "Mind telling me just who you are and what it is you're doing up here?"

"He's Katie's other husband," Mason said with a laugh as he came up behind Dak. "I have it on the best authority. Some kind of woman she's turned out to be. I never would have guessed that cute little redhead had it in—" He stopped short at the look on Dak's face. "Hey, don't blame me. She's the one who has two of you on a string, with both of you claiming to be her husband." He cast a calculating gaze on Dana. "How do you fellows decide whose turn it is?"

Dana's face whitened. "Watch your mouth, you SOB." He took a step forward.

Dak pushed him aside. "Let me take care of this," he said quietly. "Any more talk like that, Mason, and you'll find yourself minus a few teeth. Get smart and keep your thoughts to yourself. And—" his gaze locked with Mason's "—do it by yourself. Stay away from Mary Lowe."

"Okay, okay. Although I don't know why you should care when you already have Katie." Mason smiled slyly. "If you guys don't mind sharing her, who am I to..." He left the sentence unfinished when Dak started toward him, swung around and hurriedly left.

"Which brings me back to the question I asked you a minute ago." Dak took a deep breath and focused his attention on Dana. "Who in the hell are you and what are you doing up here telling people you and Katie are married?"

"Hey! You already know my name. As for the rest, you'd better ask Katie herself," Dana replied with a wry grin. "And when you find out why I'm here, maybe you can explain it to me. I'm getting a little confused."

"Yoo-hoo, Dak!" Nora Winslow called. "Come over here. We want to get your opinion on something."

Dak shook his head and waved off Dana. "We're not through talking. I'll look you up as soon as I settle this." He started toward Nora. "What's up?"

"We've decided to help you and Katie get off to a new start," she replied. "Whatever or whoever you and Katie say that man is, she needs to concentrate more on you." She gazed wistfully after Steve and smiled apologetically. "He is a handsome temptation, though, isn't he?"

"You're asking the wrong person." Dak snorted his disgust. "Now, what can I do for you?" Annoyed, but trying hard to be patient, he took several deep breaths and tried to concentrate on what Nora Winslow was telling him.

"I was saying that you and Katie need to concentrate more on each other. And we've found just the way to do it, haven't we, ladies?" she asked the other three women at the table. "Of course," she went on as she continued to stare off to where Dana was standing talking to Ellen, "while I can certainly understand what Katie must see in that man, she married you, after all. Yes, indeed," she said firmly. "You'll just have to work harder at reminding her of it."

Molly Moriarity giggled. "That shouldn't be such a hardship, should it?"

Dak frowned. Keeping Katie away from her other "husband" and out of trouble already was a full-time job. Four well-intentioned matchmakers and their romantic schemes were the last thing he needed to distract him. The way things were beginning to shape up, it looked as if he was going to be busy keeping the women happy, instead of tending to the business of securing the meeting room. Damn! He glanced around him. Keeping the ladies happy was Katie's job. Where was she when he needed her? "What did you have in mind?" he asked, even as he was afraid to ask.

"We're going to give Katie a surprise shower!" Nora announced happily. "We bought the gift while we were shopping in Carmel yesterday."

"A surprise shower?" Dak immediately abandoned the idea of letting Katie handle the women.

"A bridal shower, young man. Since you and Katie eloped, I'm sure she hasn't had one yet. Or has she?"

Dak shook his head. "I don't think so. But, to tell you the truth, I don't think she's in the mood for this one, either."

"That's precisely the point. You may have to lead a horse to water, but once it gets there, it drinks. She'll love a shower. And we want you to stay and help her enjoy it. Everything will be just fine. Trust me."

With a sinking feeling in his chest, Dak knew that a bridal shower was the last thing Katie needed or wanted. And that she wanted him around even less.

"What exactly did you have in mind?" he asked, knowing full well that if Nora Winslow wanted to give Katie a shower he wasn't going to be able to dissuade her. From the conspiratorial glances the ladies exchanged and the self-satisfied smile on Nora's face, he knew he didn't stand a chance.

"We want you to take your wife away for the morning while we make our plans."

"No problem."

"And be sure to have her back here around two."

"Right."

Dak's thoughts, as he turned away from the romantic women, were dark. He shuddered to think what Katie's reaction would be when she found herself the guest of honor at a bridal shower.

Chapter Eight

With an effort, Dak put his private feelings about his future with Katie aside. He had to find her and persuade her to spend the day with him.

He suspected that getting her to go anywhere with him in her present state of mind *was* going to be a problem. But it was his job to preserve the semblance of being a newlywed, no matter how she felt about him.

His thoughts reeling at the idea of a shower, he set off to find his not-so-blushing bride.

Ellen Fraser, waving impossibly long red nails, waylaid him. "Katie suggested Steve and I take the women out for a sight-seeing ride this morning. Do you and Katie want to come along?"

Dak shuddered. The prospect of spending the day with an angry woman didn't thrill him, but listening to romantic plans all morning thrilled him less. Besides, thanks to Nora Winslow, bless her, he had an agenda more to his own liking. Rejecting it would look suspicious. "No, thanks. I thought I'd take Katie down the coast to Big Sur for the morning."

"Take me where?"

Katie's faint scent had preceded her. She smelled of salty air and honeysuckle blossoms. Honeysuckle blossoms? How incongruous, he thought as he turned to greet her. She looked like the consummate businesswoman, but he knew there was more to her than that. The picture of her undulating belly dance popped into his mind. Her perfume should have been exotic, like her background. Something spicy. Certainly not honeysuckle, an innocent and demure scent. He associated it with swinging on his grandmother's porch, where he'd spent many a lazy summer afternoon with the little pigtailed girl next door. Whatever else Katie might be, he thought as he admired her figure, her sparkling green eyes and auburn hair, she was definitely not the girl-next-door type. More like an exciting vision out of the *Arabian Nights*.

"I thought you might enjoy a ride down to Big Sur State Park and lunch in a special restaurant I know. Just the two of us."

"Where, Dak?" Ellen Fraser moved closer. "Sounds as if it might be a more interesting way to spend a morning than a drive cooped up in the van."

Dak mentally groaned. Ellen was far too interested in his plans for Katie. He had a feeling that it wouldn't take much encouragement for the entire group to decide to follow him. They were out of luck. The last thing he needed was an assorted group of onlookers while he made his peace with Katie.

"Sorry, Ellen. Today is just for Katie and me. Besides, we'll probably be gone all day."

"Now, wait a minute," Katie protested. "I haven't agreed to go with you. After all, I have a job to do here," she said. "And so do you."

"Sure thing," Dak replied. "And that's just what I'm trying to do." No sooner had he'd said it than he realized Ellen had overheard him, that he'd given her an opening she was smart enough to catch. Damn! Katie had been right. The way he'd been behaving since they'd arrived at the Tickle Pink Inn, he *could* just have well been trained at *Spy* magazine instead of USC and the police academy.

"A job?" Ellen echoed. She considered Katie and Dak. "What a strange way to describe a honeymoon. Or is it a honeymoon?" she asked thoughtfully. She turned on Steve. "As for you, you've never told me exactly where you fit in in all of this."

Steve shrugged and grinned helplessly at Katie.

"Never mind all that," Katie interjected hastily. "I've decided to go with Dak."

"Quick, let's get started," Dak muttered. He looked over his shoulder to where Nora and the other women were approaching. "The troops are getting restless." Thank God Katie had understood the trouble they were in and had acted appropriately. He shuddered to think how close they'd come to having their honeymoon farce uncovered.

"Where *are* we going?" she questioned when Dak took her arm and rushed her out of the inn.

"To a place about thirty miles south of here, below Big Sur State Park. I promise you'll love it."

THE HIGHWAY WOUND south through tall trees and partially hidden campgrounds, along deserted ocean beaches and wooded cliffs. He pointed out an occasional luxurious home and weather-beaten cabins hidden among the trees. With the top of the convertible down, Katie's hair flew freely in the wind. He smiled when she raised her face to the sun and drew deep breaths of the crisp, fresh air.

"A whole lot better than smog, isn't it," he asked, tempted to reach out and pull her closer. She looked as pleased as a kid on the way to Disneyland, as happy as she'd been yesterday when they'd played in ocean tide pools. His heart warmed to the smile on her face. She was still a child at heart, and at times, it appeared, so was he.

An hour later, they pulled into the parking lot of a picturesque group of buildings of redwood and adobe. A worn redwood sign identified it as the Nepenthe restaurant. In the entrance, a massive redwood sculpture of a phoenix stood atop a stump of an oak tree.

Katie paused to admire the setting. "Nepenthe? What an unusual name."

"It comes from the Greek, meaning 'no sorrow,'" Dak explained. "Actually, it was a mythical Egyptian drug that induced forgetfulness and surcease from sorrow." Dak drew Katie's hand through the crook of his arm and led her into the open-air restaurant. "As for the sculpture of the phoenix, it's symbolically rising from the ashes of the tree that once stood there. I thought this place had a lot of meaning for the two of us. Maybe we can start all over again, too. What do you say?"

She was doubtful. He was obviously trying to get on a friendly footing. But after this morning, she felt vulnerable. How could she tell him how deeply he'd upset her when he'd said she'd been playacting, teasing when they'd made love. Or when he'd accused her of a one-upmanship and trying to take over his job?

Nothing could have been further from the truth. She had a romantic nature, sure, but she was selective, and delivered on what she promised. Not that she'd promised too often before Dak. She'd given all of herself to him without reservations. His mistrust and harsh words had burned themselves into her mind.

As for taking over some of Dak's job, it wasn't deliberate. Well, maybe that was her nature, too. It came from a lifetime of competing with five brothers who'd treated her as a toy. And now Dak was making the same noises, in spite of her having given all of herself to him. She was reluctant to get hurt again.

"I don't know. Why don't we take one day at a time?"

He was disappointed, and more than a little annoyed. It had taken a lot for him to apologize—twice, as a matter of fact. It just wasn't the type of thing he felt comfortable doing and he'd be damned if he'd do it again. Maybe it was for the best. Two tempers in a relationship would have been one too many. He'd had enough of that. "Sure, no problem," he said. "Let's have lunch."

The table was covered in a red-and-white checkered tablecloth. The bench seat that rimmed the balcony overlooking the ocean was covered with matching thick red cushions. A small crystal vase held spring wildflowers and bright green leaves. The pungent odor of eucalyptus trees filled the air. Soft music played in the background.

"What a beautiful place for a restaurant," Katie said in admiration. She moved to the edge of the balcony and gazed out over the ocean. "Look out there!" She pointed to a family of otters swimming along the shoreline. A pelican dove into the ocean and surfaced with a fish dangling from its bill. As if on cue, the otters turned on their backs and clapped their fins. Katie laughed. "I love it!"

"The whole Big Sur area is full of places like this." Dak smiled at the way she had come to life. "Ever changing, never the same. If we have time, I'd like to show some other interesting spots to you."

"If we have time." Katie cast a lingering glance at the shimmering blue-green ocean where the otters chased one another, dove beneath the water and resurfaced. "But there *is* the conference. As a matter of fact, I feel guilty about leaving the planners to their own devices."

"It's their job. Yours is making certain they have the tools they need and that they have their privacy. Mine is making certain the place is secure. They don't need us taking up their time." Dak handed her a menu. "As a matter of fact, we're largely along for show."

"Show! I'd hate to think that all our work is merely for show. What about the women? And Mason?"

"They're part of the show, too, even if they don't know it. Anyway, they don't need us, either. They're doing real fine entertaining themselves." A boyish grin curved his mouth. "It's just you and me, kid. Let's make the most of today. Would you like me to order?"

"Since you've been here before, yes."

He ordered a crustless quiche made with spinach, mushrooms, onions and a combination of cheeses, a side salad and sangria that arrived with slices of citrus floating in the ruby red fruited wine.

"I'll never be able to eat all that!" Katie motioned away the crisp toast and fresh-vegetable appetizers that the waitress placed on the table. "I'd be ready for bed in..." She blushed and turned away to gaze at the ocean.

"Eat what you can. I'll help." Dak politely ignored the wide-open opportunity to tease her again. In the meantime, tell me more about this puppy you're so homesick for."

She raised a questioning eyebrow.

"Yeah, I know." He found himself apologizing one more time. No one but Katie O'Connor could have moved him to do it. "I should have asked you the question, instead of sounding off this morning."

"You're right." Katie sighed. "I am homesick. McDuff is the sweetest bundle of Scotch-terrier energy you could hope for. I'd just gotten him from someone who raises them, when I had to leave to come up here. Poor little thing, he's developed some kind of puppy problem. That's why I call home every day."

"At seven-thirty in the morning?"

"Yes. That's when the vet has time to fill me in on McDuff's progress. He even has McDuff talk to me. That way I know the puppy is okay."

"Talk to you? The animal talks to you? Ask me why I'm not surprised." Dak chuckled. As a matter of fact, she did manage to surprise him, even intrigue him, with her changing personalities. Today she sounded like a vulnerable young woman. "It would be just like you to talk to dogs and believe they answer back."

"I didn't mean talk, exactly, but he does bark when he hears my voice. The vet says McDuff seems less lonely after I call."

"I guess I should have let you explain this morning, before accusing you of passing inside information to someone on the outside." Dak took a long swallow of the cool sangria and dismissed McDuff.

"But there's still the question of Steve Dana. Who is he, anyway?"

"That's something I can't discuss." Katie obviously wasn't prepared for true confessions.

"Can't?"

"Won't," she said firmly.

"Well then, have it your way. One argument a day is enough for me. Let's finish up here. I want to show you the park on the way back. I promised to have you back in the early afternoon."

"You promised? Whom did you promise and why?"

"You'll find out." Dak held his breath, afraid he'd let the cat out of the bag.

His self-conscious smile was unintentionally revealing. Something involving her was going on. An unwanted premonition swept over her. "I'm not sure I'm going to like finding out. Am I?"

"Come now. Two can play at this game. There are some things I can't discuss, either. You'll have to wait and see."

IT WAS ALMOST four o'clock when they got back to the inn. Dak figured he'd done his duty by keeping Katie away until then. He was going to make himself scarce. Attending a shower wasn't a high priority for him. Besides, he'd had it on the best authority that men weren't welcome at times like this.

"You go on to the Cliff Side Deck. I'll see you later," he said, hoping to leave before Nora spotted him.

Katie felt bewildered at the speed with which he disappeared. She couldn't understand why he was rushing away from the inn's daily afternoon wine-and-cheese happening. Something definitely was going on. For a man trained in security, his face had been a dead giveaway.

"There you are, my dear." Nora Winslow seemed to be waiting for Katie. She glanced at her three companions and put a finger to her lips before she turned back to Katie. "You're just in time for wine tasting."

"No, thanks, I've had enough wine for one day." Katie dropped into a large cushioned armchair. "I've had such a wonderful time today. But I wouldn't mind joining you for a while."

"Good." Nora beamed at her and pulled over a chair. "It sounds as if you and Dak are finally on the right track," she said confidentially. "I never did believe that other man was your husband, anyway." She paused and bent over to whisper, "He isn't, is he?"

"No, ma'am, he isn't." Katie forestalled the next question. "It's a long story, and one that I'm sure wouldn't interest you."

Over Nora's shoulder, Katie could see the staff bringing out fresh fruit, wine, cheese and crackers. She could also see a determined look in the lady's eyes. Katie closed her eyes and leaned her head against the high-backed chair. She sensed another lecture coming, but she felt too contented after a day with Dak to care.

"I'm so pleased to see that you've taken my advice. You *have* made up with your husband, haven't you?" Without waiting for a reply, Nora went on, "Men aren't perfect creatures, are they?" She sighed. "But the poor dears mean well. I complain about my Bob, but he's really a sweet man, and a good father. You've heard we've been blessed with four sons and a daughter and twelve grandchildren, haven't you?"

Katie nodded. From what she'd learned of Nora Winslow, it was evident that it was all Katie was expected to do.

"It's just a matter of focusing on your husband's good qualities, remembering why you fell in love with him in the first place."

"Of course," Katie agreed, hoping she looked suitably impressed with the advice. "I'll try to remember that."

"Good. Well, now that I've gotten that off my chest, let's get to why you're here. We have a surprise for you."

Katie sat up. Her sixth sense had been right on target. Three of the older women were beaming at her as if they were proud grandmothers. The fourth, Mary Lowe, was smiling sympathetically. "A surprise?"

"Yes. Now, you just sit back and enjoy yourself." With that admonition, Nora disappeared into the small pantry and came out with a package beautifully wrapped in white-and-silver paper and tied with a huge white ribbon.

Katie could see an interested crowd gathering. From the package's white wedding wrapping, the get-together was beginning to look suspiciously like a wedding shower. She managed a weak smile. The last thing she wanted or needed was that.

"Now, first we'll each have a glass of champagne. We're going to toast the bride." Everyone on the terrace, including the waiters, rushed to pick up a glass. "May you and Dak always be as happy as you are today," Nora said as she toasted Katie and handed her the boxed gift with a flourish. "Go ahead, open it," she commanded.

Katie looked around her at the expectant faces. If the women only knew the real state of affairs between her and Dak, they would tar and feather her, instead of giving her presents. But the Toyland wives seemed to be set on putting on a shower, with her the star attraction.

Whoever had wrapped the box had used knots known only to the U.S. Navy and Coast Guard, Katie thought grimly as she struggled with the tightly wrapped ribbon. She finally reached for a knife on the serving table beside her and cut it in two.

"Dear me. That means you're the next one in line to have a baby!" Nora announced to general laughter.

Katie muttered. The sooner she opened the present, the quicker she could get out of there. She lifted the cover, unwrapped layer after layer of white tissue and extracted a brief white satin undergarment. It was a minuscule teddy that looked as if it were intended for a Barbie doll. One glance and she hastily replaced it in the box.

"Go on!" some cheerleader in the crowd called. "Let's see what else is in the box."

Blushing madly, Katie noticed another garment of bridal gossamer white satin and sheer silk. The satin teddy had a matching robe. Designed to reveal rather than conceal, neither one could possibly have covered more than an inch or two of skin. Good heavens, she thought as she gazed thunderstruck at the gift stickers on the box. Victoria's Secret!

Certain that she was crimson from the tip of her head to her sandaled toes, Katie hastily rewrapped the gift. Around her, her audience broke into laughter. There was a smattering of applause. Smiling weakly, she thanked the women, backed out unto the terrace and headed for her suite.

SHE CLOSED the door behind her and took a deep, calming breath. The first free breath she'd been able to draw for the past hour. The bridal shower, complete with a cake that had been followed by wine, crackers and cheese and fresh fruit, had been almost too much for her to handle. Knowing all the while she was an imposter, she'd been kept busy accepting congratulations and good-natured advice. The ribald comments that followed the opening of the box containing the teddy and the robe had surely been more suited to a bachelor party than a bridal shower. Cringing inside, she'd played along for the sake of the masquerade. The shower and the gift had been an experience she hoped never to have to experience again.

She threw herself on the bed. Willed herself to relax. Eyed the half-open box she'd tossed onto the mauve-and-gray bedspread. Now that she was alone, she could appreciate the good intentions behind the bridal shower, could even see the humor of the situation without wanting to cry. Thank goodness Dak hadn't been there to witness her humiliation. It would only have given him more fuel for his sexual innuendos. She'd had enough of those to last her a lifetime.

The white gift box, with its contents, was a temptation she found she couldn't resist. Glancing around to make certain she was alone, she slid off the bed and lifted the robe from the box. She left the teddy behind in its tissue cocoon. Even now she couldn't look at it without blushing. She couldn't imagine anyone, even a new bride, wearing such a garment on her wedding night.

The urge to try on the sheer white robe was irresistible. She took off her outer clothing, put on the gossamer confection and moved to the mirrored door that led to the bathroom. With its high collar, which framed her auburn hair like a halo, the garment was a study in sheer elegance. There were no buttons, only a series of white satin ribbon ties from the neck to the waist. She ran her hands down the silky material, shivering as it slid against her skin and through her fingers.

On an impulse, she swung into a graceful belly dance. The sheer material swirled around her like a fleecy white cloud. She felt so feminine, so womanly. If only Dak had really been her husband. She stopped thinking. It was no use teasing herself, fantasizing a wedding night with him. She was only a make-believe bride, with two fake husbands, one hired, the other one masquerading as her husband to get even with her. Neither one was real . . . or belonged to her.

"Don't stop now," a voice whispered behind her. "I don't think I could stand it if you quit."

Katie froze. In the full-length mirror, she could see Dak lounging against the door frame. His hands were thrust in his pockets; his avid gaze seemed to devour her.

"On the other hand," he said as he cleared his throat, "I don't think I could stand much more of this if you continue."

He straightened and slowly came toward her. "Who are you, Katie O'Connor?" he asked as he took her chin in his hand and raised her face to his. "I never know who I'm going to encounter next."

"I'm just Katie," she murmured, her eyes locked with his.

"Never 'just Katie,'" he answered, lowering his lips to hers. "Oh no, never *just* that."

He gathered her in his arms, turned her around to face him. He pushed aside the collar of the robe and kissed her nape, the hollow at the base of her throat. Lingered at the swell of her breasts. His lips triggered a wave of desire, made her stomach flip-flop, brought tears to her eyes, a breathless sigh to her throat. She offered him her mouth, her breasts. His scent drifted over her as he kissed her without realizing he was bruising her lips. He kissed the tips of her breasts through her sheer robe. Reason fled as he whispered tender words into her throat, blew softly into her ear and gently outlined her ear with his tongue.

Katie was dimly aware of the pulse that throbbed at the side of her neck. The strength of the arms that held her. And Dak's body heat, which matched her own. No matter that he was a make-believe husband. He belonged to her now.

She caressed the back of his head as he leaned down to kiss her. Wanting more, she held his lips closer to her breasts. Willed him not to stop. He murmured his approval and bent to his task. She rubbed her tongue along her lips, bruised lips gone dry with passion. Closed her eyes, the better to feel him all around her.

"You don't need this, Katie."

She heard his whispered words of admiration as he untied the row of satin ribbons that held the filmy robe together and slid it from her shoulders. He snapped open her bra and lifted it from her. Her bikini panties followed. Holding her away from him, he ran his hands over her naked flesh.

"You're all silk and satin without it."

Chapter Nine

Katie had expected to awaken in Dak's arms. To relive the hours they'd spent loving each other, to love again. To tell him the whole story behind Steve Dana's appearance. To share a laugh over her having hired a husband, instead of accepting Dak when Gibson had first suggested it. Instead, his side of the bed was empty. Not even a trace of his body heat lingered.

Hoping to find a note telling her where he had gone, she searched the bed covers. Nothing. A glance at the empty chair alongside the bed told her he'd dressed before he'd left. Disappointed and feeling lonely, she pulled the sheet over her nude body and settled back to wait.

Half an hour later, she decided she'd been fooling herself. She meant nothing to him, was merely another woman in a long line of conquests.

How could she have fallen into his arms so soon after telling him they were no better than strangers? And how could she have let herself be taken in by him?

Her glance fell on the bridal robe from Victoria's Secret. It lay on the floor in a frothy puddle where he had tossed it last night. The white gift box containing the robe's matching silk-and-satin teddy lay beside it. Heat suffused her when she recalled Dak's telling her she didn't need to wear the robe or the teddy to arouse him, that she was sexy enough without them. And his typically male remarks about the teddy getting in the way on a wedding night.

Angry at herself for her reaction at finding him gone, Katie slid out of bed and kicked the offending box under the chair. She wadded the robe into a tight ball and knocked it out of the way. How naive she'd been to put it on and not expect him to react when he'd found her wearing it. She should have realized he was liable to come into the suite at any moment and that she was asking for trouble.

As far as she was concerned, she muttered as she headed for the bathroom, the maid could have the cursed robe and the teddy, too.

Half an hour later, she'd showered and dressed in her comforting, shapeless blue sweats and tied her hair back in a ponytail. Feeling more like her old self, she put on her Reeboks and prepared to exorcise Dak's lovemaking from her mind. A hard three-mile run around the landscaped grounds should make her feel human again. After that, she was prepared to seek out Dak and tell him exactly what she thought about the games he was playing. She'd tell him what he could do with his male hormones. And when she got through with him, he'd damn well better understand that they wouldn't be sharing the bed again.

FEELING PRETTY satisfied with himself, Dak made his way into the suite, juggling a loaded teakwood breakfast tray. He'd had to wait for the bakery delivery, but the scent of the croissants told him it had been worth it. In addition to the warm buns, fresh orange juice, a small jar of whiskey marmalade and pats of fresh butter, he'd wrangled a split of champagne and a crystal vase containing a single red rose. Since he had plans for a special interlude with Katie before breakfast, he'd skipped the hot coffee. He'd make some later with the suite's coffeemaker. Out of consideration for her confessed weakness, he'd even passed up the offer of a thermos of hot chocolate. Laying the tray gently on the coffee table, he walked carefully to the bedroom door.

The last he'd seen of Katie, she'd been curled around the pillow that appeared to be her permanent bed partner, even after he'd taken its place. It had taken determination on his part not to kiss those beautiful parted lips before he'd left the suite, to kiss her awake, to watch the sleep leave her incredible sea green eyes as she welcomed him into her arms. He hadn't had the heart to awaken her. Not when her porcelain complexion and halo of auburn curls had made her look like an innocent, sleeping child.

He laughed happily. Who was he kidding? Last night and the night before, she had demonstrated she was more than an innocent child. She was a highly desirable woman who was creeping into his heart as surely as if she'd been shot there by Cupid's arrow.

Aglow with his special plans for himself and Katie, he couldn't wait to awaken her.

He carefully pushed the sliding door aside. To his dismay, the bed was empty. Frowning, he checked the room. Why hadn't she waited for him to come back? Surely she should have known how much she'd pleased him, how much he wanted her again and again. He'd planned to brush her lips, her breasts with the dew-kissed rose. To follow its downward path with his own lips. To inhale her sweet scent. To take up where they'd left off last night.

He perked up when he remembered her exercising in front of the mirrored bathroom door. Recalling the movements that had resembled a sensual belly dance more than exercises made his body stir. He cautiously opened the door on the chance she was in the bathroom practicing again, or taking one of those long, hot soaks she seemed to love so much. The room was filled with steam—and empty.

She'd been there, all right. Showered and left. Puddles of water led from the shower. A damp robe was thrown carelessly on the floor. Frowning, he turned back into the bedroom and stumbled over the large white gift box that protruded from under the chair. It was then he noticed the bridal negligee wadded into a ball. He picked it up and ran his hands lovingly over the frothy, silken material and thought of her warm, soft skin.

What the devil had gotten into that redhead this time? he wondered as he reviewed last night. After hours of loving, she'd fallen asleep in his arms, her head tucked into his shoulder. The last thing he remembered was her smile. The night had been wonderful. So why wasn't she here waiting for him this morning?

Ignoring the breakfast tray that sat on the coffee table, Dak strode out of the suite, through a side door and out into the rain-swept grounds. He headed for the cottage at the rear of the property he knew was occupied by Steve Dana. Nestled in a small clearing, and hidden amid the pine trees and colorful flower beds, it was a perfect lovers' hideaway.

It occurred to him that if he'd known of the cottage's existence when he'd registered, he would have requested it for Katie and him. It was wasted on the likes of Dana, unless she was there with the guy.

Angry and deep in thought, he slid off the slick path of aged boards that made up the walk between the cottage and the main building. Before he could recover his balance, he stepped into a mud puddle of standing rainwater up to his ankles. Disgusted, he took off his shoes and socks, rolled up his jeans and set off again in his bare feet. Even though the mishap wasn't Dana's fault, Dak added one more mark against the man he considered his rival for Katie's attention. And who, for all Dak knew, might even be an industrial spy.

Still barefoot, he stepped gingerly up the cottage stairs and pounded on the door until Dana opened it. Dressed in partially buttoned jeans, Dana looked as if he'd just tumbled out of bed, and none too happy at the interruption.

"Where's Katie?" Dak demanded.

"I'll bite. Where *is* Katie?" Dana answered, rubbing sleep from his eyes and squinting at the rising sun. "Good Lord, it's hardly daylight!" He glanced at the muddy shoes Dak carried and down at his mud-covered feet. "What happened to you?"

"Never mind. I want to talk to Katie. I know she's in there."

Steve lost his sleepy look. "I told you I don't know where she is. You're not coming in here."

"That's what you think. Now, step aside if you value those made-for-TV looks."

A woman's voice broke in. "Katie's not here."

Dak looked over Dana's shoulder—Ellen Fraser.

"Katie's not here," she repeated. "If you can't keep better tabs on your wife, don't expect Steve to do it."

Dak grimaced and, grateful that his instincts had been wrong, held out his hand. "Sorry, fella. Maybe I'm out of line, but Katie *did* bring you up here with her. And she *has* been seen with you in the dead of night."

Steve shook Dak's hand. "That's okay. If you're really Katie's husband, I guess I don't blame you for being worried about her. As for Katie bringing me with her... well, I just don't understand what kind of games you people are playing."

"Games, huh? Well, I intend to find out myself as soon as I locate that redheaded bundle of trouble," Dak muttered as he started down the steps. "That, and a whole lot more."

"Hey, wait a minute." Steve called him back. "Maybe I should help you look for her. In a way, I feel responsible for Katie."

"In a way?" Dak stared up at him. "What way is that?"

"Well, I am her husband, of a sort."

"Of a sort?" Dak couldn't believe his ears. "Are you or aren't you?"

"I have a signed contract saying I am," Steve answered with a cautious look on his face.

"A contract? How about a marriage license?"

"Er... no."

"Then forget it, mister. And keep away from her from now on."

"But what will she say? After all, she's the one who's paying me."

Dak shrugged. "I'll take care of Katie. Just as soon as I get my hands on her." She didn't know it yet, but the marriage game with Steve Dana was over. Not that he'd tell her he knew about the masquerade just yet. It would be more satisfying to play dumb for a while longer and see how deep a hole she'd dig for herself.

"Do you want me to go with you and help you look?"

"No, thanks. Just send her back if she comes up here. And remember what I said. Keep away from her."

Dak made his way back to the inn. He was just in time to bump into Katie as she jogged around the corner of the building.

"Where the hell have you been?" he demanded, his concern for her safety turning into anger now that he'd finally found her.

"I might ask you the same question!" She planted her hands on her hips and glared back at him.

"I went to get us breakfast and had to wait around until the bakery delivery. When I got back, you weren't there."

"Yeah, sure. Some story. You had to have been gone for at least an hour or more before the time I woke up expecting to find you in bed. You didn't even have the decency to leave a note telling me where you were! Under the circumstances, I didn't think I was required to wait for you to come back."

His eyes narrowed as he took in her rumpled blue sweats and her Reeboks—the outfit she wore when she was trying to fade into the landscape. No matter what alibi she might come up with, it looked to him as if Katie were up to her old tricks. He wanted to grab her and shake the truth out of her. And not only for reasons of security. Didn't she realize how worried he'd

been when he couldn't find her? "And just where did
you go?"

"None of your business," she retorted as she
pushed past him and headed for the inn. Where was
the trust that should have blossomed between them
after a night of loving again? Where was the man with
whom she'd crossed the boundaries of a mere relationship? "You can't intimidate me, mister. Two can
play this game."

The coffee table was empty when Katie jogged into
the suite with Dak close behind her. Through the open
sliding doors to the bedroom, she could see the bed
had been made up and fresh, dry robes hung on the
door to the bathroom. The sheer negligee she'd tossed
away was draped gracefully across the bed. She felt
herself blush. What must the maid have thought when
she'd found the negligee on the floor?

"You did say you went to bring breakfast back?"
Katie asked as she tore her guilty gaze from the sen-
suous-looking garment and pointedly glanced around
the suite. "For a man in your profession, you could
have thought up a better excuse than that."

Dak studied the empty coffee table. "I didn't dream
it up. I did leave the tray on that table. It was there
when I left to look for you."

He went to the telephone, dialed the housekeeper's
number and barked his question into the phone. "Oh.
No, that's all right. Hold on a minute." He offered
Katie the phone. "Would you like to have housekeeping explain what happened?" When she shook her
head, he spoke into the phone. "We'll eat later,
thanks.

"Seems that the housekeeper saw us each leave the
suite and figured she'd have the room straightened up

by the time we got back," he explained. "I never thought you'd be up and gone before I brought back breakfast or I would have left you a note. So, now that you know I was telling the truth, what do you have to say for yourself?"

Katie worried her bottom lip. Tried to meet his eyes, but couldn't. If he wasn't smart enough to understand how she'd connected his disappearance with his earlier accusations and how miserable she'd been to find him gone, she wasn't going to explain it to him. "Maybe I shouldn't have reacted the way I did, but you needn't talk to me as if I'm a child. Even if you think you have an apology coming, I'm not going to make it. Not when everything about the way you're behaving tells me you still suspect me of some kind of crime, that you still don't trust me."

"Katie, I was only joking about the apology," he stammered. "I thought we'd gotten close enough for you to know where I was coming from."

"Too close, but obviously not close enough for you to trust me." She folded her arms around her middle and stood her ground.

"Well then, if you won't buy that I was teasing you, surely you can understand that the way you've been behaving is off-the-wall. It's my nature and my job to wonder what you've been up to. How can I trust you completely when you've lied to me from the very first about being married and Lord knows what else?"

"How can you make love to me feeling the way you do?" she countered. "No, you don't need to answer that. I've heard trust has nothing to do with love-making. That where men are concerned, love needn't enter into it, either." She eyed him coolly. "It appears I heard it correctly."

She turned and walked into the bedroom before he could answer.

THE TOYLAND contingent were making good use of the breakfast bar when Dak and a subdued Katie arrived. Her plate piled high with fresh fruit and warm croissants, Nora Winslow smiled at the newcomers.

"How are the newlyweds this morning?"

"Come on, Nora. Leave the kids alone. You're embarrassing them," her husband said. "Finish your breakfast and let's get on with the day."

"I don't know what it is about the cooler climate up here in Carmel," Nora said with a laugh, "but I'm so hungry I could eat a bear. How about you, Katie? If I remember correctly, being a newlywed sharpens the appetite," she continued, ignoring her husband's exaggerated groan in the background.

"Thank you, but no, thanks. I've already eaten." Katie glanced at her watch and smiled halfheartedly at the incurably romantic Nora. "Goodness, it's almost nine," she said meaningfully in an aside to Dak.

"Hal and Pat have already gone to see if the boys can go fishing again," Nora offered with a sigh. "I don't know what the fun is in fishing if you don't catch anything to eat."

"Today's gonna be different, luv," her husband said as he patted her on her ample shoulder and kissed her cheek. "I promise you we'll bring back enough fish for the chef to make up for dinner."

"We'll hold you guys to that," Dak replied. He applauded Winslow's quick thinking. And unless he misunderstood his cue, it was now up to Dak to find a fishing pier and a willing lucky fisherman while the men were at their meeting—and to see that the purchase would be served at dinner.

"Why don't you come along?" Richard Lowe asked. "Even a new groom deserves some time off for good behavior."

Dak made a show of glancing down at his brown chinos and beige turtleneck. "Sorry, I'm not dressed for it. Besides, I don't think Katie would appreciate my leaving her alone, being a new bride and all that. You guys go on. Katie and I will think of something interesting for everyone to do."

"The aquarium in Monterey!" Nora announced. "I've heard so much about it—we'll all just have to see it."

Dak exchanged glances with Katie, hoping she'd refuse to go along so they could talk out their problem. He felt troubled, but not entirely discouraged, when she quietly agreed to go. He intended to settle their differences on the way up to Monterey, and not only by talking. There were a number of places where they could stop and park on the beach. Where he could take her in his arms and show her how much he regretted their misunderstanding.

As far as he was concerned, that's all it was—a misunderstanding. Except for the answers to a few more questions, he was almost ready to believe that Katie was just what she appeared to be: a well-intentioned and hardworking woman. A little too precocious for her own good, but he was ready to overlook that, too.

"Dak, why don't you arrange for tickets while I see if Ellen and Steve can drive us up there in the van?"

He frowned and started toward Katie to tell her he was going to drive the two of them to Monterey. That he wanted to be alone with her. That he didn't want to have to share her with anyone else today. The warning look in her eyes stopped him. He reluctantly nodded his agreement. "I'll be back in a few minutes."

He ran down a flight of stairs to the terrace, took the boardroom key out of his pocket and turned on the conference room's lights. At the first glance, everything looked in order. Except... When the short hairs on the back of his neck started to tingle, he scanned the room. He strode rapidly toward a landscape painting that hung on a wall. Last night when he'd locked the room, he'd made certain the painting was perfectly aligned, that the safe containing their precious drawings behind it was closed and secured. Now the painting was slightly askew, as if it had been hurriedly rehung. For the first time in three days, something was wrong.

Dak carefully lifted the framed picture from the wall and checked the wall safe. It was securely closed. But the notch on the dial pointed to the number thirty-nine, not twenty-four, the number it should have been. No wonder he'd felt the hairs on the back of his neck vibrate in warning. His worst suspicions were confirmed.

Thirty-nine! Every night when he locked up, he put the day's computerized drawings and other papers in the safe, closed the door and twirled the dial before he left it pointing to a special number. Having started with twenty-one, his lucky number, each night he added one more number. Three days later, it should have read twenty-four, not thirty-nine!

He held his breath as he dialed the secret combination that would unlock the safe, then flung the door open. The contents were stacked neatly inside, just as he'd left them last night. But there was no doubt in his mind that someone had tampered with the safe. He strode back to the door and examined the lock. It didn't look as if it had been forced, but as far as he was concerned, that didn't mean anything. He could be dealing with a clever thief, or else someone who had access to a key.

He felt a sense of betrayal. While he'd been loving Katie, the mice had been at the cheese. He'd have their tails in a vise if he caught up with the thieves. No, when he caught the thief, he was going to damn near kill the culprit before he turned him over to the long arm of justice. While possibilities ran through his mind, he settled down to wait for the conferees to show up.

One by one, dressed in full fishing regalia, the men drifted into the boardroom. Cynthia followed closely behind them carrying her paints and portable easel.

"Damn, it would be nice if we could actually go fishing this morning," Bob Winslow complained. "Herb told me they're really biting up at Moss Landing."

"Yeah. Maybe we could skip meeting tomorrow morning and go fishing, instead," Hal Morton agreed. "I know it would clear the cobwebs out of my mind."

"Hold up, fellows. We've got a problem." Dak stopped the conversation.

"What kind of problem?" Winslow demanded as he dropped his fishing pole in a corner. "Just what in the hell are you talking about?"

"In a minute." Dak swung his gaze to Cynthia Mason. "Cynthia, you're usually the last one to see copies of the day's computerized blueprints for the new toy you're working on. Did you have them yesterday?''

"Of course. But they were only preliminary drafts. Nothing's been finalized, you understand. Hal gave them to me to look at after he'd printed them, so I could start planning color schemes.''

"Were they far enough along to identify them as being a toy?'' When she nodded, he shifted into high gear. They were in trouble. "What did you do with the drawings after you were finished with them?''

"I left them on the table so you could store them in the safe. Just as I usually do. As a matter of fact, I'm sure you were the one who put them in the safe when you came back in to lock up. After all, you're the only one with the combination.'' Cynthia dropped her paints on the table and joined Dak at the safe. "Why?''

"Wait a minute. Just what's going on here?'' Winslow elbowed his way between them. "What's happened?''

Patrick Moriarity took off his fishing hat and peered over their shoulders at the open safe. "Something missing?''

"Could be.'' As he'd been doing for the past twenty minutes, Dak ran his hand through his hair in sheer frustration. By now he was sure he probably looked like a porcupine at full alert. "Damn, how could this have happened?'' He gazed around the silent group. When no answers were forthcoming, he gave up. "Well, there's no use beating a dead horse. Let's take seats and examine what we do know.'' He took out the annotated drawings from the safe and lay them on the conference table. "Let's go through the blueprints one by one. Bob, since you're the designated group leader, how about filling me in on your progress yesterday. I didn't get a chance to ask you after I came back from spending the day with Katie."

"Blast!" Winslow sank his bulk into a chair. "Gibson will have our jobs if this one gets away from us!"

"Hold on a minute. Let's find out what's missing, before you start collecting unemployment insurance."

Dak spread the papers on the table. "Here's everything that I found in the safe." He passed the eight-and-a-half-by-eleven sheets along, one by one— drawings that eventually would become the toy on which Toyland was staking its future. "Check these and tell me if you're missing anything. Anything at all."

He watched while the drawings were scrutinized and passed around the table.

"Nothing's missing that I can tell," Winslow finally said as he threw the last of the drawings on the table. The others murmured their agreement.

"Someone was in the safe," Dak declared, suppressing his impotent frustration. He needed a clear head if he was going to get to the bottom of this. "I'm willing to bet on it."

"How come you're so positive if everything seems to be accounted for?" Richard Lowe asked. "Especially since we all agree that everything is here."

"I'm as positive as I know the sun will set tonight." Dak sank back in his chair and looked around the room. He wasn't about to give away his secret method of setting the safe combination. "What I'm not sure about is who did it. But we all know what they were after."

He took a last glance at the drawing on the table. "Well, let's get started so you can get to work."

Dak reached behind the bar that stood in the corner of the room and punched in a special code on a recessed lock. The bar swung aside to reveal a small well-hidden closet. Two Toyland computers, several cellular telephones, a copier and a laser printer were stacked neatly to one side. He carried one of the computers into the conference room and plugged it in. Patrick Moriarity and Hal Martin brought out the other items.

Dak went back for the cellular telephones, closed the secret door and put the telephones on the bar that reappeared after he'd punched in the secret code again. "Now, don't forget to encrypt your calls. And keep an eye on all the documents! Don't even destroy copies. Save them for me. I'll take care of them when I get back from the aquarium. I'll also want to know where everyone was last night."

Just what each of them had been doing last night? He hoped no one would be crass enough to ask him that question. If they did, he'd stand on his honeymooner's right to privacy. Insist on his rights under the Fifth Amendment to the Constitution. Kid around about being a new bridegroom. Anything. His nights with Katie were too precious to share. The days—well, the days were turning out to be something else again.

"Surely you don't suspect one of us!" Hal exclaimed. "What would we have to gain? What the hell, our jobs depend on Toyland's success."

"And hefty stock options, too," Pat Moriarity reminded him.

"Nevertheless," Dak said firmly, "I'll want to talk to everyone later. I'll see you all this afternoon."

"Going out to play while we do all the work?" Cynthia said to Dak's back, her voice loaded with sarcasm.

"That's what honeymooners are supposed to do, enjoy each other." Dak shrugged her off with a hard look over his shoulder.

"I wouldn't know. Ed's been an SOB from the day we got married."

And Cynthia Mason was no Miss Innocent from what he'd seen so far, Dak privately observed as he closed the door behind him. Although it was none of his business, her behavior toward her husband turned him off. And Ed's roving eye, which had settled on young Mary Lowe, didn't sit too well with Dak, either. If ever a couple were a misfit, it was the Masons. But he wasn't going to let them bother him. Not now. He had a bigger problem to worry about.

He tried to shake off a growing feeling of disquiet and concentrate on more pleasant subjects. Getting back on neutral grounds and making up with Katie were the most important things on his mind, but even they took second place.

What bothered him was that, to his knowledge, he and Katie were the only ones who had a key to the boardroom. And he was the only one who knew the combination to the safe. Unless, by some means unknown to him, Katie had obtained the combination to the safe, too.

Chapter Ten

Dak left the grim-faced toy planners behind as he grappled with this unsettling thought.

It troubled him to think that Katie of all people might be capable of sabotage. Worse yet, he couldn't imagine her as a woman who would ransack a safe. But something was going on. The combination to the safe had clearly been tampered with. He'd thought of dusting it for fingerprints, but he'd left his equipment behind at Toyland.

Besides, whoever had been smart enough to figure out the combination to the safe had probably been smart enough to wear gloves. As for Katie, if she'd taken anything, it hadn't been obvious when he'd met up with her. Unless she'd hidden it under her bulky sweatshirt.

Was it guilt that had made her react so strongly when he'd confronted her this morning? How else could he explain her anger? At the time, his questions had had nothing to do with the possible theft of the blueprints, anyway. Hell, she should have realized he was upset because he'd been worried about her safety.

The pragmatic side of him told him Katie might be involved, even if he didn't want to believe it. He'd gotten over his suspicion that she was using code words when she made her phone call at precisely seven-thirty every morning. But there still were doubts. Maybe no one was as perfect as she appeared to be. Maybe she *was* up to blackmail. Or, she could have intended to pass inside information to her brother. After all, he *was* a stockbroker and could specialize in insider trading in the toy industry. As for Katie herself, Dak knew she'd worked for a distributor before she'd come to Toyland. She was sure to be acquainted with many people connected with the industry. For all he knew, she could have been planted at Toyland by a competitor. The personnel department should have checked her out more closely when she'd been hired.

And then there was Steve Dana. Unknown to Katie, he *could* have been a cleverly introduced industrial spy. From the speed with which he'd connected with Ellen Fraser, Dana could easily have sweet-talked her out of a key to the boardroom.

Ashamed at how far his imagination had gone, Dak hated the idea of his Katie being an industrial spy.

His Katie! The idea was so new it took him by surprise. Good Lord, when had he started thinking of her as "his?" How far could this "bonding" stuff have gone, for Pete's sake!

He was shocked that he actually enjoyed every moment of their combative relationship. Losing himself in her arms for the past two nights had been the best ever. He'd probably told her so. But, he thought as he carefully searched his memory, he didn't remember promising her anything. Or had he? Maybe that was why she was so angry with him.

The fact remained that she'd gotten to him in a way he couldn't explain. He knew only that he looked forward to being near her; to enjoying her quick mind, her lovely body; to touching her, holding her. Even if their relationship was more like riding up and down an emotional roller coaster.

She always seemed to take him by surprise. It made him feel as if every hour together was an adventure. He only hoped that the adventure hadn't suddenly become dark and dangerous.

THE SPOUSES were waiting for him when he finally made his way to the parking lot this time. Today Ed Mason and Steve Dana were ready to go along. Dak cursed under his breath. As if he didn't have enough troubles already. It was all he needed to completely mess up his day.

"Come on, Dak, hurry up," Nora called. "The aquarium opens at ten. I don't want to stand in line."

"I don't think we'll have to, Mrs. Winslow," Ellen reassured her. "The tickets you bought here at the inn will let you walk right to the head of the line."

"Oh good! Waiting always makes me so hungry." Nora hesitated. "Maybe I'd better take along an apple or two, just in case. Now, Dak, you hop right in back there alongside Katie. I'll be back in a minute."

Dak tried to be patient while he watched Nora hurry back into the inn. Tried, but failed. He took a dim view of a half-hour drive with eight other people packed in a pink van. Having to breathe in and out in unison set him to seething inside. He wanted Katie to himself where they could talk privately, just as he'd planned. He tried to catch her eye, but she looked away.

He studied the others in the group while they waited. Looked for unusual signs of stress. All he got were smiles from the women and raised eyebrows from the men. If anyone of them was guilty, he or she sure knew how to hide it.

He wanted to ask each of them what they'd been doing last night, but couldn't see how he could bring it up without causing comment. He'd have to wait until it came up in conversation.

They finally set off, with Ellen driving, Nora beside her, bending her ear, and Mason in the jump seat. To Dak's disgust, he, Katie and Steve were squeezed into the back seat, with the other three in the middle seat. He wouldn't even be able to carry on a private conversation with her. Not with Steve only an inch or two away.

Katie closed her eyes and tried to divorce herself from the situation. With Dak's body against her, his arm thrown over her shoulders to give them enough room, she could sense his displeasure. Well, she wasn't too happy about the arrangement, either. She'd had enough of his proprietary air, his macho ways. Not to mention the way her body kept betraying her whenever he was close.

She stirred restlessly as she thought about last night and the night before. She recalled the passion in his hazel eyes as he'd gazed down at her. And the weight of his nude muscular body pressing against hers. The magic in the hands that had stroked her to fulfillment. And the sensuous mist that had enveloped her afterward.

As if he intended to remind her that he was there, Dak rubbed his knee against hers.

She could pinpoint the change in both of them to the minute. It had been when he'd held her close while they were dancing and hummed a love song into her ear. Some spell had taken hold of her. She'd been able to feel the strength of his arms around her long after the dance was over. She felt it still.

The past two nights in his arms had been heavenly. More beautiful than she'd ever dreamed possible. Until this morning when she'd awakened alone. Disappointed, and unsure of herself, at first she'd thought that he'd cared far less about their new relationship than she had. That he was the "love 'em and leave 'em" type. Maybe she'd been wrong, but his reactions when he'd come across her jogging hadn't reassured her. He still mistrusted her. Knowing that she'd given him sufficient reason by claiming Steve as her husband didn't help. It just reinforced the feeling that when the conference was over their relationship would be over, too.

Dak sensed Katie's inner turmoil when her body stiffened and she drew away from him and moved closer to Steve. He saw Dana throw him a puzzled glance before smiling uneasily and shifting to make room for her. Dak even knew a burst of jealousy when Katie smiled up at Dana and murmured her thanks.

Jealousy, for crying out loud! He never thought he'd live to see the day when he was actually jealous. And not just because Katie had accused him of it. Hell, he'd declared his independence from women the day he'd gotten his divorce. But then, he realized with a pang, she was a different kind of woman. He took a kind of perverse satisfaction in knowing she was his wife—for this week, at least.

"Okay, everyone, we're here. You go along inside while I park the van," Ellen announced after a ride that seemed to Dak to have lasted an eternity. "I'll go look for a parking place." He was pleased to see Dana hop back in the van and go along with Ellen.

Once inside, he took Katie's arm and, before she could protest, managed to lose Nora and the others in the crowd. He led her through a large exit door to where there were tide pools and sea otters to watch.

"We're going to talk, Katie," he said firmly as he guided her to a secluded bench. "And we're going to start at the beginning."

She sighed. "Okay, talk. Although I don't know what else there is to say after this morning. I seem to remember we said it all."

He took a deep breath and plunged right in. "Someone's been at the safe where we store the working blueprints of the new toy."

That got her attention. Her eyes widened in disbelief, then horror, as the implications dawned on her. "Good heavens! Do you realize what that could mean?"

"I realize, all right, and it scares the hell out of me. I'm going to question everyone when we get back to the inn, but I thought, under the circumstances, I'd talk to you first."

"Under what circumstances?"

"Well, we *were* together all last night."

Katie looked away. He could see a blush rise over her neck and cheeks. He felt a little warm himself. "The way I figure, the safe was tampered with sometime after I locked up last night and before nine this morning. Since there were people around everywhere until after midnight, my best guess is that it happened sometime before dawn this morning.''

"Before dawn this morning," Katie repeated slowly.

Her blush disappeared, and as what he was saying sank in, her skin tone turned white. Moving almost in slow motion, she gazed quietly at him. Too quietly.

"So that's why you were so angry this morning!"

"No," he countered. "What kind of a man do you think I am? At the time I didn't know anything about the tampering of the safe. I was worried about you."

"And more than a little suspicious, I'll bet," she answered with a look that should have frozen him in his socks.

"Not about this, I swear." He said a silent prayer that she wouldn't ask him why. He was already in enough trouble.

She seemed to let that pass for the moment.

"But now?"

Her eyes were loaded weapons as, if knowing the answer, she frowned at him, dared him to accuse her. If looks could kill...

"Come on, Katie. I didn't find out about the breaking and entering until just before we left for the aquarium. I haven't even had a chance to interrogate anyone yet."

"So you thought you'd start with me as the most likely suspect, is that it?"

"Seemed like a good place to start," Dak answered carefully. "After all, you do have a key to the meeting room."

"And?"

He had second thoughts when he saw the hurt in her eyes, but it had to be said. "It occurred to me that you might even know the combination to the safe."

Katie surged to her feet, disturbing an inquisitive baby sea otter that had swum to the edge of the tide pool to investigate the intruders. "You're absolutely right. I do have a key to the meeting room. As for the combination, how would I know it? Unless you were talking in your sleep!"

She took him by surprise. "*Do* I talk in my sleep?"

"No, you moron! I heard a lot of malarkey from you when you were awake, but none of it was the combination to the safe!"

The startled baby otter barked his distress at the shouting. Katie paused in her tirade, shot Dak a quelling look and bent down to reassure the mammal. "Don't worry, sweetheart. We won't hurt you. If anyone gets hurt, it's going to be this idiot. I may even cut him up in pieces and feed him to you for lunch."

The baby sea otter barked its approval, rolled over on its back and clapped its fins.

When the otter finally settled down and turned its attention to him, Dak smiled in grim amusement. No matter that he was many times its size, the little devil seemed ready, willing and able to take him on.

No one but his Katie would think of such a mind-boggling threat to intimidate him.

"Okay, Katie." He knew he had a choice. Believe her or not. Work with her or against her. He threw up his hands in surrender. "Now, curb that temper of yours, come back here and let's put our heads together."

Katie sniffed. "Not until you tell me what was really bothering you this morning. You *did* say that at the time you hadn't gotten around to suspecting me. So, what was the problem?"

His pride kept him from admitting he'd been jealous of Steve Dana. Nor was he ready to reveal that he pretty well knew where Dana came into the picture. "Let's face it. Maybe we were both guilty of nothing more than venting our wounded egos. You because you thought I'd abandoned you, and me because I thought last night didn't mean enough to you to have you waiting to welcome me back."

"Perhaps." She dismissed him with a disdainful toss of her head. "And now that we're on the subject—" her irate gaze locked with his "—you've finally gotten around to thinking I was in the boardroom when I was out jogging, haven't you?"

"The thought has entered my mind." He took a step backward when he saw her reaction. "After all, you were coming from that direction. But I'm willing to believe you if you say you didn't do it."

"That's big of you. Now that we know neither of us broke into the room, who else has the key besides us?"

"Mrs. Fraser, but I've discounted her."

"Why? Because she's your number one fan?"

"Come on, give me a break. You're the one who picked the Tickle Pink Inn for a meeting place, not me. It's highly unlikely Mrs. F. would have anything to do with industrial espionage. Of course," Dak said thoughtfully, "some people will do anything for money."

"They would have to have known what we were actually doing up here in the first place, wouldn't they?" she reminded him. "And I didn't tell anyone."

"That makes it between the fellows and Cynthia and us. Unless you told Steve. Did you?"

Katie rummaged in her purse. "Where's my pen-knife," she muttered. "I'm going to cut you up in little pieces and feed you to the otters now."

"Okay, okay." Dak laughed again when the otter swam up to the edge of the pool where he was standing and seemed to be waiting for Katie to carry out her threat. "Let's agree we're both clean. When we get back, I'll call everyone together and have it out."

She looked a trifle mollified. "Seems to me no one is going to confess to anything, especially if you just come right out and ask them," she said. "They'd have to be crazier than you are. I think you should do some of your supersleuthing, instead. I'll help," she said firmly.

"I'd rather you didn't."

"Come on. When the others have a chance to think about it, they'll realize we're the only people with a key, and maybe the only ones who know the combination to the safe. No, forget I said that. I *do not* know the combination," she hastened to add when Dak's mouth opened. "If you'd get off your manly duff, you'd realize we're in this together."

Chapter Eleven

"Now that we've settled that," Katie remarked briskly, "is there anything else you wanted to talk about?"

Dak was too engrossed by the way she looked silhouetted against the sunlight to answer her question. Curvy where it counts, she was appropriately slender everywhere else. In her lime green suit and daffodil-colored T-shirt, she appeared like a spring wildflower. And now that she'd gotten over her anger, her green eyes sparkled with good humor. He couldn't help himself; she was as pretty as a picture and twice as cute. Even the little sea otter seemed to be lost in admiration as it cocked its head and continued to gaze at her. Either that, or, heaven forbid, it was waiting for her to carry out her threat and provide him for dinner.

"Dak?"

"Sorry, what was that you said?" He tried to pull himself together and get back to business.

"Is there anything else you wanted to ask me about?"

Startled out of his preoccupation with her appearance, he tried to focus on her question. "No. Not right now."

"Then let's see some of the other exhibits." She blew the little onlooker a goodbye kiss. Its whiskers twitched, but its large, expressive dark eyes continued to watch her every move. When it didn't budge from the edge of the pool, Katie sighed. "Oh dear, I don't think it's going to leave before it gets its dinner."

While Dak listened in disbelief, she carefully explained to the otter that she'd given him a second chance. After throwing Dak a look that he would have sworn was one of disappointment, the hungry mammal finally shook its head, barked its disappointment and glided away to find another meal. "It's so cute I wish I could have taken it home with me," Katie said wistfully as she watched it disappear.

It took Dak less than sixty seconds to make up his mind about what to do next. "Go on ahead and wait in line over there by the theater. They're showing a movie on Monterey Harbor and its grand canyon. I'll catch up with you in a few minutes."

"Where are you going?" she asked. "I don't want to get separated from you." She blushed when he glanced at her under raised eyebrows. "Oh! Meet you later."

He was amused at Katie's discomfiture as she hurried away. He didn't intend to get separated from her, either. Not in the aquarium or anywhere else. He had an important agenda, all right, but it wasn't what she thought. He waited until she disappeared from sight and made his way into the aquarium gift shop. He had something very special in mind for her and he wanted it to be a surprise.

Dak rejoined her just as they opened the door to the theater for the next showing. "Later," he whispered when she glanced at the small shopping bag he carried.

Fifteen minutes later when they filed out of the theater, he caught her eyeing the bag again. It was okay with him; he couldn't wait another minute to see the expression on her face when she found out what he had bought for her. "This is for you," he said as he handed her the gift. "To celebrate our latest truce. And to give you something to remember it by."

"The paper is so beautiful I hate to unwrap it," Katie remarked as she took out and turned over the package. "Will you look at all the fish and the sea mammals. There are even little sea otters!"

"Yeah, including a picture of the one who thought I came to dinner," Dak said, chuckling. "Unwrap the package. I think you'll like what's inside."

She carefully unwrapped the gift and drew out a white T-shirt. A trio of little sea otters, whiskers and all, gazed back at her with soulful eyes. "Oh, Dak! What a sweet thing to do!" Impulsively she threw her arms around him and planted a kiss on his cheek.

He wasted no time. Drawing her aside into a more secluded place against a pillar, he clasped her face in his hands and kissed her back. But this time with all the pent-up frustration that had been building inside him. Maybe better than words, he reasoned as he brushed his hard lips against her, this would show Katie how he felt about her.

The intensity of his kiss took her by surprise. Remembering the morning's quarrel, she pulled back and studied him carefully. The cold, cynical Dakota Smith had vanished as if by magic, replaced by a tender man, sensitive and comical enough to understand her love of animals and, yes, even of sea otters. Sensitive enough to buy her a shirt with a picture of their own little hungry mammal on it. He'd found her tender spot, all right. She decided she was going to take things more cautiously this time, instead of plunging in where they'd left off.

Thinking it was, after all, only a kiss and nothing more, she leaned into his arms, savored the taste of him, the feel of the hard-muscled arms that pressed her to him. She kissed him back with all the pent-up desire inside her, a kiss that unleashed a storm of passion between them. The world seemed to turn upside down; the two-story exhibit tanks vanished in the sensuous haze that spread over her. The defensive walls she'd tried to build around her heart crumbled under Dak's determined assault.

"I can't believe that you bought me the shirt even after I threatened to cut you up in little pieces and feed you to the otter for dinner," she said, laughing shakingly when he let her come up for air.

"Consider it another apology," he answered, smiling into her eyes and outlining her swollen lips with a gentle forefinger. He kissed her again, this time at the corners of her mouth. "Okay?"

"It's awfully public around here," Katie said when she finally tore herself away from him and caught her breath. Behind her, there was a burst of applause. Glancing around at the interested onlookers, she colored and buried her face in his shoulder. "Good heavens, people have noticed us. Maybe we should get back to the inn and back to business."

"Oh, I intend to," he whispered into her nape.

"Serious business. Just as soon as we get back to our suite."

His words set her good intentions into a tailspin. If only she could believe he'd come around to trusting her. If only their relationship wouldn't keep waxing hot and cold. That it wasn't merely built on the obvious physical attraction between them. That he cared enough for her to believe in her. "I only meant we should get back to the business of finding out who tried to break into the safe."

"Broke into the safe," he corrected, nuzzling her cheek with his lips.

"Whatever you say, as long as you don't think I'm the one who did it. Stop that," she said with a laugh when he nipped at her ear. "I can't think clearly when you're acting this way."

"Neither can I," he agreed. "But there's really no need to think. And frankly, I can do this with my eyes closed."

The amused glances of passersby were forgotten as Katie lost herself in his demonstration.

THE CONFERENCE attendees were waiting in a tight-knit group around the bar when Dak and Katie arrived after finally managing to persuade Nora Winslow and the others to return to the inn. Positive that they never would have gotten Nora to come back if they hadn't held out the promise of the bounteous wine-and-cheese served every afternoon, Dak signaled the attendees to meet him in the boardroom.

Grim-faced, Winslow regarded Katie with a jaundiced gaze when she appeared at Dak's side. "Thought this was going to be a secret meeting," he declared. "No offense, Katie. It's just that I was under the impression the idea was to keep this whole thing quiet until we solved the puzzle of the missing drawings and blueprints.''

''If there are any missing blueprints.'' Cynthia Mason shot to her feet and glared at Dak. ''So far, no one has been able to prove that anything's missing. I personally think Dak likes to invent a melodrama so he can play heap-big detective. And furthermore, I'm tired of waiting around until he decides to do something about it.''

''Now, that's just like a woman,'' Hal Martin said in disgust. ''Everything becomes a personal attack.''

''Come on, everyone. This isn't going to get us anywhere.'' Richard Lowe paced the floor as he spoke. ''But the truth is, Dak, outside of talking about your gut instinct, you haven't told us why you think something's missing from the safe.''

Dak studied the reluctant and puzzled participants for a long moment. The time had come to reveal the truth. In addition to not wanting to give away his secret methods, he hadn't wanted to involve Katie. Hell, the truth was he had no choice. The secret was out. In fact, all the secrets were about to come out unless he figured out a way to deflect questions.

Dragging Katie into this would bring up questions about Steve Dana, who he was and what he was doing here. So far, everyone had treated Steve's appearance as a joke on Dak, but as sure as hell would never freeze over that was about to end. With two men claiming to be her husband, even if Katie didn't become a suspect, she was bound to be a target for some nasty gossip—if she wasn't already. And, he thought with a sinking feeling, Neil Gibson would hear about it. From someone like Cynthia.

He exchanged a resigned glance with Katie, motioned her to a chair and walked to the head of the conference table.

"Okay, everyone, lighten up. I'm about to tell you my secret. Not that it stayed a secret very long," he added bitterly. "Sure as hell someone's figured it out." He went on to explain the method he used to close the safe's combination.

"Seems to me that it just took some persistence to find the right combination," Hal Martin announced. "As an engineer and a sometime computer hacker, I probably could have figured it out if I'd set my mind to it."

"A computer hacker? Just what Toyland computer programs have you infiltrated?" Bob Winslow demanded to know. "Sales figures?"

"Lord, no. I just play around with the software programs. Not often, you understand," he protested as the rest of the group regarded him with suspicion, "just once in while. I like to keep my hand in the technology. I just do it for the fun of it."

"It's against the law!"

"Come on, Bob. I would never use the info."

When they all started talking at once, Dak pounded the table with his fist. "Come on now! First things first. I for one am not interested in Hal's secret life. If he says it's a harmless hobby, I'm willing to believe him. Katie, you take notes and let's get started. I'll want to know where each of you were after midnight last night and before nine this morning. Let's start with Cynthia."

"That's discrimination, I'll have you know." Cynthia sat up in righteous indignation. "I was in bed, if it's any of your business. My time from nine to five may belong to Toyland, but the nights belong to me!''

"That's one down," Dak announced, motioning to Katie to take notes. "At least you're not claiming sexual discrimination. If you are—" he leaned across the table and eyed Cynthia coldly "—forget it.''

He glanced over to where Katie sat scribbling on the yellow notepad. Auburn tendrils framed her serious face as she bit her lip in concentration. Damn, but she was lovable! He wanted to get finding the thief out of the way so he could get back to making love to her and finish cementing their bond.

"There's nothing sexual in the way I feel about anyone but Katie" he found himself saying as he watched Katie raise her head and blush.

When Cynthia tossed her head, the men guffawed. Satisfied, Dak continued. "Bob, you're next."

"To tell you the truth, I was in bed pretty much of the time. Except for when I went out to the candy machine to get a pick-me-up for Nora.''

"Did you see anyone else wandering around?''

"No. Not that I can remember.''

"All right. Patrick?''

"I was in bed where I belonged. Molly takes this second-honeymoon stuff seriously.'' Patrick Moriarity threw up his hands. "I wouldn't risk leaving until after she woke up and found me there.''

In the background, Dak heard Katie sniff. So Katie wasn't the only female who wanted her man around after a night of loving. He wanted to laugh, but didn't dare. Instead, he chalked the information up for future use.

"Richard?''

Richard Lowe gritted his teeth and lowered his gaze to his clasped hands. "In bed," he said.

After a short silence, Winslow sat back in his chair, cocked his head and glanced from Dak to Katie and back again. "I guess it's your turn now. What were you and Katie doing last night?"

"Come on, Bob." Dak hastened to get in between any questions that might be directed at Katie. "We're newlyweds, for crying out loud. What do you think we were doing?"

"Nora mentioned that you and Katie have had a quarrel a day since you came up here. By the way," he said, laughing, "you'd better watch your step. Nora plans on doing something about putting romance back into your marriage. Brief as it is."

Dak remembered Katie appearing disgusted when she'd told him about Nora finding her in the hall at midnight the first night of the conference. That she'd indeed lectured Katie about how to keep a husband happy. He uttered a silent thanks to Nora Winslow for not telling her husband and casting more suspicion on Katie than there was already.

Dak decided to rush right in where angels feared to tread—no matter how much he might hurt Katie in the process. He had to hurt her to save her, he figured. He'd explain later. "Did you ever know a redhead who didn't have a mind of her own?" he offered. When no one replied, he went on. "Bet you didn't. Anyway, Katie's no exception. She doesn't like my bossing her around. At least, in her interpretation of my bossing her around. But—" he cast a wicked grin at a thunderstruck Katie "—it's pretty cool making up."

The four men seated around the table seemed to silently regard him with new respect. Dak took one look at Katie and realized he'd better apologize to her as soon as possible. He was prevented from doing so when Cynthia laughed bitterly.

"How like a man," she said.

Winslow brushed her comment aside. "Yeah, but the fact remains that you and Katie are the only ones with the key to the room. And from what you tell us, you're the only one with the combination to the safe."

"That seems to be the case." Dak nodded reluctantly.

"Well then, I hope you understand where I'm coming from. Since we can all account for where we were last night, and you two are the only ones with keys to this room, I guess it's up to you and Katie to prove that you aren't the guilty parties. Yeah, I know," he said as Dak started to protest, "but as group leader, it's my job to get to the bottom of this before any damage is done."

"You're absolutely right." Dak rose to his feet and walked over to put a protective hand on Katie's shoulder. "And it's my job to supply the answers."

DAK WANDERED to a far corner of the inn's grounds. He found a gazebo covered with blooming honeysuckle vines and surrounded by masses of spring flowers. A padded seat ran around the inside. Secluded, with the interior hidden from view by the climbing vines, it was just the place to plan their investigation of the theft.

"We can talk privately here," Dak said after he'd checked their surroundings. Something in Katie's expression made him take the notepad from her, drop it to the ground and pull her into his arms. She tried to look away from him, but he knew better. He had hurt her, and he couldn't bear the wounded expression in her eyes.

"Katie, you aren't upset over what I said about your being a redheaded shrew, are you? I didn't want anyone to ask you anything that would embarrass you. I just intended it to be a red herring, to keep you from being questioned."

"I know, but it still hit home. It was one of the things you said to me when we first met."

"Blast!" He cursed himself as he recalled their first meeting. Sure he'd said that, or at least intimated it. And, to his regret, he'd said it more than once. No wonder she couldn't trust him. She still thought he didn't trust her!

"Katie, sweetheart," he said as he stroked tears away from her shimmering green eyes. "I don't really think you're a shrew, I swear. You can't deny that you're a redhead, sure, but take it from me you're a damn sexy one. And, I confess, a lot smarter than I thought you were when I first met you. As a matter of fact," he said as he punctuated each word with a kiss at the corner of her lips, "I love more than just your looks. I'm even beginning to believe that you're a lot smarter than I am."

Katie tilted her head to one side and, through the foolish tears that still threatened to fall, regarded the tender expression on Dak's face. Remembering the angry, disenchanted man who had railed at the thought of a honeymoon inn and at her for thinking of it, she forgot her own unhappiness. "That's quite a confession, coming from a man like you. I've never thought about who was smarter. It's just that I've wanted to feel as if we're partners in this assignment.

I felt put down by what I thought was your patronizing attitude.''

"I hope you still don't feel that way. Do you?" Dak asked as he kissed his way down her neck.

"No, I guess not." Who could think at a time like this?

"You guess not?"

"I'm sure." Katie shivered when Dak kissed the hollow between her breasts. "Very sure. If I wasn't, I'd probably have kept my promise to the sea otter."

"Oh, Katie! You are a wonder!" He lifted her in his hands, twirled her around the gazebo and dropped onto the cushioned seat with her in his arms.

"Don't forget we have a mission to accomplish," she reminded him when he started to unbutton her blouse."

"I know. And I'm about to get started."

IT WASN'T until after they'd returned to their suite and she'd showered that Katie was able to pull herself together long enough to get down to business.

"I've been putting together some of the pieces in the Toyland puzzle. I remember seeing Ed Mason prowling around the grounds late at night. Maybe he's the guilty one."

"Say that again?" Dak strolled out of the bedroom, toweling his hair.

"I said I remember seeing Ed Mason out on the grounds late at night."

"When you were out prowling yourself?"

"I wouldn't put it that way exactly. I was just out."

Dak dropped the damp towel on the floor and sank onto the couch beside Katie. "Now that you've brought up the subject, just what way would you put it?''

Katie blinked. Asking for blind trust in her was one thing, Dak's wanting the truth was another. She thought about it for a minute. After reviewing the change in their relationship, she decided he was entitled to know the facts. Prepared to tell him everything, she took a deep breath and started.

''Steve Dana isn't my husband. Never was.''

''Got it.'' Dak struggled to keep a poker face. ''True-confessions time?''

''If that's what you want to call it. I hired Steve from a husband-for-hire service that turned out to be in San Francisco—The Harrington Agency. I heard about it on a radio talk show after I turned you down. When I knew I had to have a husband I flew up and hired Steve. Actually, the agency telephone number is an eight-hundred number. I didn't even know where the agency was when I called. I had to produce a husband fast, and it was the most likely source.''

Dak nodded. It figured, even if getting a husband through a radio commercial was something only his Katie would think of doing. ''Go on,'' he said encouragingly. ''Did you know Steve before you hired him?''

''No. And he'd never heard of me, either. I was shown his picture on a computer screen. He's a local TV soaps actor between jobs and seemed to fit the bill.''

''With his acting ability,'' Dak remarked, trying, but not succeeding, in controlling a laugh, ''he's probably between jobs a lot.''

"Not at all. I think Steve's doing pretty well, under the circumstances. Mrs. Fraser thinks so, too. And Ellen."

"That explains who Steve is, but not what you were doing out on the grounds in the middle of the night," Dak prompted. "Although I guess Steve's played some part in it?"

"I was only trying to keep out of your clutches. I figured the only way to do it was to spend the nights in his cottage. But after he discovered Ellen, which was right away, thanks to you, neither he nor the cottage seemed to be available to help me out. In fact, the night of the storm, he insisted I go back to our suite and to you."

"Thank goodness for that!" Dak happily remembered the storm and its aftermath. "Do you realize what the guy could have read into your strange behavior? Especially when he obviously doesn't seem to know what the hell the caper is all about?"

"Now you're jealous again! I should have never told you about him."

"Jealous, my eye. Steve impresses me as being all male, and you're definitely all female," Dak remarked as he gazed at the portions of delicate pink skin that escaped from under her bathrobe. "He would never have been able to keep his hands off you if you'd spent the nights with him."

Katie grinned her satisfaction. "I love it when you're jealous. Shows you're human."

"I'm human, all right. Come here." He grabbed her around her waist and pulled her across his lap before he realized his mistake. There was no way he could keep his mind on the subject of Katie's hired husband as long as she was so close. Especially after her robe fell open a little farther and a few more inches of pink skin was exposed.

She scrambled out of his lap, laughing. "I really think it's time for us to get down to making a list of the rest of the suspects in the case."

"So, Steve and Ellen are off the list?"

"Yes," Katie answered as she consulted her notes. "And probably Bob and Nora, too. He's been with Toyland too long and has too much to lose to sell it out now. As for Nora, the darling doesn't seem to be interested in much besides me and you. And where her next meal is coming from. But I don't discount Ed Mason, or his wife, either. And while we're at it, I'd like to know more about what Richard and Mary Lowe were doing last night."

"Yeah, I didn't buy Dick's answer, either. He acted too uptight and frustrated when I asked him what he had been doing. If anything, he should have been angry at my asking such a personal question. But he wasn't."

"I made a note of it," Katie said smugly. "Lots of notes."

"I'll bet you must have attended detective school and graduated at the head of the class, Katie O'Connor. It doesn't look as if you're going to need to leave any 'sleuthing' to me."

Obviously pleased by the compliment, she beamed back at him. "Don't worry. We're partners, aren't we?"

Dak liked the way she was able to turn her complete attention back to the possible theft of the blueprints, even when temptation, namely him, was staring her in the face. The ability to keep one's mind on a problem under stressful conditions was the mark of a true professional. First things first, in the order of priority, was every real detective's motto.

She'd changed a lot from the first time he'd met her. He remembered the take-charge businesswoman. He thought about the lengths she'd gone to hire Steve Dana. And her frustration when he had registered them as Mr. and Mrs. just as Dana was announcing *he* was her husband.

He had to give her a lot of credit at the way she'd caved in when cornered and had agreed to bunk with him. Even if she kept disappearing in the dead of the night.

Yep, she'd changed all right. And, as a matter of fact, so had he.

His thoughts drifted back to Cynthia, his ex-wife, and their turbulent marriage. For the first time, he was willing to admit that he had probably been just as much at fault as she had been. That she might have been so adamant about not compromising simply because *he* had been so controlling, so determined to take charge.

He was uneasy with his thoughts, but, faced with the truth embodied in a petite, vulnerable redhead, he felt the revelations about himself come fast and furious. Some of them not too pretty.

He glanced over at Katie, still making notes. Her attention had gone back to the subject of the possible missing blueprints. In her own way, she'd taught him a lot about himself. He'd changed since he'd met her, and he liked to think it was for the better. As he recalled the heartfelt smile she'd given him a few minutes ago, he knew he'd passed some kind of test. But there were bigger tests to come, and he knew it.

Chapter Twelve

"The first thing we need to do is search everyone's rooms, and then ... " Katie's voice trailed off as she saw Dak's raised eyebrow. "Sorry." She smiled as she apologized, and glanced back at her notes. "I guess I was doing it again, wasn't I?"

It was time for her to let go of the lifelong habit of competing with five older brothers. To let go of thinking she had to prove herself, prove that she wasn't just someone's little sister. If she and Dak were to be equal partners in this operation, the least she should have done was to ask him, instead of telling him.

She rephrased the question. "You do agree that we need to search the rooms, don't you?" She knew she'd said the right thing when a smile curved at the corners of his mouth and he nodded his agreement.

"And just how do you propose we do that without anyone noticing?" Dak asked.

"I thought we could do it when everyone's away having dinner!"

"It's too big a risk," he replied after a moment's consideration. "You never know when someone might take it into his head to go back to his room. Besides, it means searching five suites. We couldn't possibly do all that in one night."

"You're right." Katie frowned at her notes. "Maybe we should make a list of the likely suspects and start by searching those rooms first. We can ask Steve to keep a lookout for us."

"You sure you want to involve him?"

She smothered a smile at his question. No matter how hard he tried, Dak couldn't hide his jealousy. It never failed to surprise her that he needed reassurance that Steve meant nothing to her. She was secretly flattered, but the way she saw it, such jealousy interfered with Dak's objective thinking. "I'd say he's already involved, wouldn't you? Besides, since I'm certain he had nothing to do with the theft, he's the logical one to help us."

"Unfortunately," Dak answered with a wry grimace. "But you'd better think carefully before you decide to ask him to help us. With half the inn's staff and guests believing the guy's your husband, and the other half wondering where I fit in, you've already got your hands full without getting any more involved with him."

He was right again. For a woman with ostensibly two husbands, she had a shaky enough reputation as it is. "I think we'll have to risk it," she finally decided. "We have to start somewhere, and as far as I'm concerned searching the rooms for missing blueprints is the right place to begin."

Dak started to protest. He changed his mind when he replayed the moments of truth he'd confronted in the past hour. Not knowing when to compromise had already brought him enough trouble to last him a lifetime. He studied the determined expression on Katie's face and vowed never to make that mistake again. Learn to compromise, he told himself. One of them had to give, and it might as well be him.

"Tell you what," he said. "Let's run over the suspects one more time. We'll search the suites of the team members who can't be eliminated. That ought to save some time. And—" he paused to let his point sink in "—if you still want your hired husband to help, it's okay with me."

"Good!" She flashed him a grateful smile. "Now, let's see who's first."

He watched the play of expressions across her face as she studied her list. As she sat forward to make annotations, her robe parted. Her slender neck and one beautifully contoured shoulder appeared as the robe fell away and exposed an even greater expanse of silken skin. Mesmerized, he followed the robe's journey. When she raised her arm to push tendrils of damp hair away from her forehead, the robe made another descent and even more of her creamy flesh was exposed. And along with it, the tempting valley that lay in between.

He swallowed hard. Playing detective had its place, but not at a time like this.

"Katie," he said cautiously. "Do you suppose all this could wait until tomorrow?"

"Tomorrow?" She started to protest, until she noticed the expression on his face. She followed his riveted gaze down to where the robe had fallen open over her one breast. "Oh my!" she said as she hurriedly pulled it together. The royal blush that spread like wildfire through her made her feel like a marshmallow melting over a hot flame.

"I think we'd better get dressed so we can get to work, don't you?" She realized her mistake when he rose from the couch in one fluid motion and came toward her with a determined look in his eyes.

"Frankly, no," he said. "I can think of a number of things I'd rather have us do."

"You can?" In the first flush of desire that overtook her, Katie dropped her notes. "You look like trouble, Mr. Smith. Don't forget, we still have business to attend to."

"Trouble?" He halted in front of her and swept her with a lazy smile. "Just exactly what is your definition of trouble?"

Katie knew trouble when she saw it, and it was headed her way in the guise of a sexy lawman. From the way she'd reacted to the invitation in his eyes and the sultry swing of his body as he reached for her, she knew she was willing to get into trouble as much as he was.

"Maybe finding the thief tonight isn't all that important, after all," she answered as she dropped her notes and came into his arms.

"THIS HAS GOT TO STOP." Katie sighed as she rummaged in the dresser drawer for clean undergarments. "I really intended to do first things first, you understand. We'll never find the culprit at the rate we're going."

"Ah, yes. The first commandment for a good detective," Dak pronounced as he donned his slacks. 'First things first.' His hand brushed hers as he reached over to get a pair of socks. Seeing his things next to hers in the drawer left him with a comfortable feeling. They were like an old married couple, he thought complacently. Examining the thought, he realized he'd never felt that way before. And that he liked the feeling.

"You know," he said as he stopped to check his Mickey Mouse watch, "we have plenty of time. If it's any interest to you, everyone is probably on the way to dinner but us."

"Oh dear." Katie looked troubled. "They'll wonder where we've gone to. Now we're going to draw attention to us."

"Come on, don't be so naive." Dak laughed. "Who's going to wonder why a pair of newlyweds skip dinner?"

Katie colored. "I just wish this weren't such a public honeymoon."

"I felt the same way at first," he agreed as he stopped to kiss her in passing. "But this honeymoon seems to have grown on me."

"Me, too," she confessed. "Give me a few minutes while I comb out my hair. By the way, I'm starved."

"How about my calling room service and we'll grab a sandwich while we decide what to do next?"

"Great," she called over her shoulder. "This time, order me a big, juicy hamburger and all the trimmings. I've given up dieting. Besides, all this activity has made me hungry."

"Activity?" Dak questioned with a knowing wink. "You mean to tell me that Nora's right? That making love leaves you hungry?"

"I was talking about playing detective, Mr. Curiosity!"

He could hear her singing a fractured version of Melissa Etheridge's latest hit rock song. Something about him being crazy for her.

There was no doubt about it, Dak thought as he put on a clean shirt; he *was* crazy about this woman. Nuts about her fey way of thinking, the way she talked, the way she walked. And even about the way she sang off-key. He paused in front of the mirror to straighten his shirt collar and found himself whistling along with her.

This new partnership they'd entered into sure had a lot of things going for it, he decided, feeling pleased with himself. Especially since it gave him the chance to legitimately spend all of his time with Katie.

"We'll round up Steve and have him keep a look-out for us while we search the rooms," he said when Katie joined him.

"Where shall we start?" She handed him her prioritized list.

"Let's do the Martins'. He's an engineer and a computer freak and probably the one most likely to know how to crack a safe. He seems as straight as an arrow, but you can never tell about guys like that."

"No, you can't," Katie agreed. "At this point in time, I suppose everyone is suspect. Present company and Steve excluded, of course," she added hastily. "But there *is* something bothering me and I can't quite get a handle on it. Not when you keep distracting me."

"I've got it!" She announced suddenly. "It's Ed Mason!"

"What's Ed Mason?"

"He's what's been bothering me! I remembered seeing him out on the grounds on both of the nights I was getting fresh air."

"Fresh air? Is that what you call sneaking off to Dana's cottage?" he teased. "Getting fresh air?"

"Yes! With you making all kinds of innuendos, it was getting too hot here in the suite. And furthermore, I intend to follow him again tonight after it gets dark. After you talk to Steve, you can search the Martins' suite by yourself while I'm gone."

It was then that Dak realized Katie was dressed in her working uniform: navy blue sweats. "You can't go prowling around by yourself. It's liable to be dangerous!"

"Don't be ridiculous. I'll be perfectly fine. Where's my hamburger?"

"Coming." Dak felt equally adamant. "You're not going out there by yourself." He relented when he saw her lips tighten, her eyes narrow. He had a feeling that if he wasn't careful, he might be fodder for the sea otter yet. "Okay. Tell you what. We'll both go out there. Searching the rooms can wait for another time. You take one side of the grounds and I'll take the other. That way we'll cover more territory and I can keep an eye out for trouble."

"And if you find it?"

"I'll holler. And if you find it—" he fixed her with a stern look "—you holler."

"Well okay, if that's the only way you want it."

There was a light knock on the door. Dak opened it to room service and stood aside to allow the table to be wheeled in. He smiled indulgently when Katie removed the chrome covers to the serving plates and dug right in. "You were hungry, weren't you?"

"I never say anything I don't mean. Now, come and eat. We have work to do."

"It's still far too light. Mason's not likely to prowl until after dinner. My guess is that we have at least another hour before it gets real dark. Besides, if you still intend to get some more of that midnight 'fresh air'—'' he winked meaningfully ''—we'll have to wait a few hours. In the meantime, I have a few things I'd like to check.''

When Katie sighed in rapture over her hamburger and waved him on, he picked up the day's newspaper and turned to the business section. A quick glance at the prices of Toyland and other companies told him there hadn't been any movement in the toy manufacturers' stock prices. He heaved a sigh of relief. If there had been a leak about Toyland's search for a toy that would set the industry on its ear, it wasn't reflected in the market. He made a mental note to ask Bob how far along they'd gotten in their planning.

''Katie,'' he said cautiously, ''how's your brother doing?''

''Which one?'' she asked as she polished off a plate of fries.

''The one who's a stockbroker.''

''Oh, you mean Sean. Rich and happy since he switched to the commodities market. He's made a bundle. Why do you ask?''

Dak wasn't prepared to tell her the real reason: that he thought her brother might have been an inside trader in the toy industry. Before he could think of a reason that wouldn't anger her, a bolt of lightning flashed across the open patio doors, followed by a sharp clap of thunder. Good, Dak thought. He had Someone on his side. ''Looks as if there's going to be another storm. Sure you want to go out?'' When she nodded, he groaned.

''Another one of the detective school's commandments?''

''Of course. A good detective never gives up.''

Dak gave in. Apparently Katie had been a diligent pupil and had learned all her lessons. Too well.

FLASHLIGHT IN HAND, Katie carefully crept alongside the walkway to where she'd seen Ed Mason wandering two nights ago. There was something about the man she couldn't stomach, she thought as she lay in wait for him. And not only because of his caustic relationship with his wife. He was a sloth, a hanger-on and, from what she'd seen, a womanizer. From the little Dak had told her, one of the perpetually unemployed. Which left him time to chase anything in skirts. And the skirt he had his eye on, unless she missed her guess, was Mary Lowe. As the vulnerable young wife of a man more than twice her age, Mary had to be his prime target. Disgusted, Katie couldn't think of one good reason Cynthia Mason clung to that marriage.

Katie darted behind a hedge when she heard the sound of footsteps headed in her direction. A man walked past her, whistling as if he didn't have a care in the world. Jaunty footsteps gave him away. It was Ed Mason.

She started to follow him, when she bumped into a tall, handsome figure. Steve Dana!

"What are you doing here?" she whispered. "You were supposed to be on the lookout to see if anyone was following Dak or me."

"I don't know what you're talking about, and I'm not sure I want to know. I've had enough problems since I signed up with you and you brought me up here. I don't need any more. Come on," he said as he took her around her shoulder, "let's get you back to your room. It looks as if it's going to rain at any minute.''

"Let me go, Steve," she said, straining to get out of his arms. "I'm on the trail of something important."

"No, you don't. It appears to me you're on your way to the cottage again to spend the night, and I'm not going to have any part of it. Not with your husband keeping an eye on me." He turned her around in the direction of the inn. "Go on back to him, Katie. Forget your differences. The guy doesn't seem to be all bad."

He pushed her ahead of him along the walk. "Besides, I've got a date with Ellen," he said with a exasperated laugh. "If you'll only let me get to it."

"Let me go or I'll holler."

"Yell away. As far as I'm concerned, I'm one husband too many, and I'm about to resign," he said as he nudged her along.

Katie decided to keep her peace. If Dak hadn't found Steve and explained the setup to him, maybe it wasn't up to her to tell him what she was doing and why. Not until Dak agreed. She'd learned her lesson. She'd just have to wait until Steve left her alone and then make her way back to where she'd heard the footsteps. She looked over her shoulder. "I'm going, I'm going. You go along to Ellen."

Another streak of lightning lit up the sky. Overhead, there was a clap of thunder, followed by large drops of rain. "You sure?"

"I'm sure." Katie waved Steve away and ran for the back entrance to the inn.

Over her shoulder, she saw Steve hunch his shoulders and make for the entrance to the building where Ellen and her aunt had a suite. As soon as he was out of sight, she turned around and headed for the place she'd last seen Ed Mason. She could just make out his pale outline disappearing in the rain ahead of her. Just as she thought, he was headed for the gazebo. Hidden by the bushes, she crept after him.

"JUST WHAT in the hell are you doing out here?"

Steve froze at the sound of Dak's voice. "Oh no!" he said, shielding his eyes from the rain. "I don't know what I've done to deserve this. First Katie and now you. So help me, all I did was answer a casting call for a hired husband, and it's been bedlam ever since! If this wasn't so far from L.A., and me without a car, I'd tear up the fool contract and light out of here so fast it would make Katie's head swim!"

"Relax. Where have you been? I was looking for you earlier."

"Ellen and I went into Carmel for dinner. Why?"

"Oh, nothing. It's too late to explain anyway. It'll have to wait until another time. Say, have you seen Katie?" Dak asked as he swept the grounds with his flashlight. "We've gotten separated."

Steve breathed a sigh of relief. "Then you don't think we were together?"

"Nah. She explained all about hiring you. But I am worried about her wandering around out here by herself."

"In that case, go back and look in your suite. I bumped into her and sent her home a few minutes ago."

"Good show. I owe you one." Dak clapped Dana on his wet shoulder and took off at a run for the inn. He skidded to a stop when he heard someone hissing at him. Sure enough, off to his right and hidden behind some bushes, Katie was beckoning to him.

"I found what I was looking for," she said in an exaggerated whisper. "Ed Mason."

"Never mind about Mason just now," Dak scolded as he contemplated her soggy sweats and rain-drenched hair. "You're sopping wet. Don't you know when to quit?"

"I told you I never quit."

"Yeah, I know. A good detective never quits," he growled as he grabbed her around the shoulders. "But another commandment to remember is that there's a time and place for everything. And this isn't it!"

"Quit shoving," she said as she dug in her heels. "I've got something to tell you."

"Tell me later. I want you inside where you can dry off."

"No way. It always turns into something else. Not that there isn't a time and a place for that, too." She dimpled at him through the rain. "But this isn't it, either."

Dak knew he was licked. "So, what's this about Mason?"

"Don't you think it's odd that he sneaks around at night? If something is really missing, it could be Mason who opened the safe and he could be passing the blueprints to someone else right now!"

"Hell...pardon the language, but I'm soaked clear through and I'm beginning to feel like a water buffalo. I ought to have my head examined for being out here in the first place." Knowing that she wasn't going to give up, he grabbed her hand. "Okay, if you're sure you know where Mason was headed, lead on."

They made their way to the gazebo and, when they heard the sound of voices, hid behind a clump of bushes.

"The honeysuckle vines are too thick to see through from this distance," Katie whispered. She tried to find a place where they weren't so abundant, but all she got for her efforts was scratched fingers.

"Thank God for big favors," Dak responded. "I'd hate to think that anyone saw us when we were in there."

"I'm going to get closer and try to see what's going on." Katie bent low to the ground and made for the vine-covered structure before Dak could stop her. Cursing under his breath, he followed.

He could hear the sound of Mason's voice coming from the gazebo. It was too low to make out what he was saying, but from the tone of his voice, the guy was definitely making a sales pitch. Feeling like a fool, Dak inched closer to where Katie had parted the vines and was peering through them. From the shocked expression on her face, he was almost afraid to look.

Ed Mason had Mary Lowe in his arms. His voice cajoled her; his hands caressed her. "Relax, sweetheart," he said as he tried to kiss her lips. "You know you've wanted this as much as I do. Let me show you what you've been missing."

"I'm not sure about continuing this, Ed. My husband..."

"Your husband is an old man," he finished for her. "And probably fast asleep by now. He needs his rest. You, on the other hand, need someone young like me to show you what loving is all about."

"Love!" Katie sniffed. "That man doesn't know the meaning of the word."

"Shhhhh! They're liable to hear you!" Dak whispered.

When Mason bent to kiss Mary in the hollow between her breasts, Dak grabbed Katie and pulled her away.

"There's your thief, Madam Detective," he murmured. "But I don't think they're talking about blueprints, do you?"

Katie shook her head. "No," she said mournfully. "I sure wish we could do something to stop them before Mary gets hurt."

"Mary's a big girl now." Dak squeezed her shoulders in sympathy as he hurried her through the darkness. "Who knows, maybe this isn't the first time she's had an affair. Maybe that's the reason for the bitter and angry tone in her husband's voice when he said he'd spent last night in bed. He probably did, but what he didn't say was that he was alone."

"You're right. So, who's next on the list?"

"That's my girl." Dak tried to console her. He knew what it felt like to have a pet theory blow up in your face. "Do you remember the true detective's motto? Never give up?"

She stood on tiptoe when they reached cover and lifted her face to his. "You ought to know me better than that. Tomorrow night we can start searching everyone's room. Tonight we have some unfinished business to take care of. I may postpone things for a while, but I never forget and I never give up."

"Neither do I." Dak's voice held a fervent promise as he gathered her into his arms and strode with her through the driving rain to their suite. "I plan on holding you to that."

"HERE, LET ME help you out of those wet clothes," Dak offered when Katie became entangled in the top of her wet sweat suit. The soaked cotton material stubbornly clung to her arms and head, but below... Dak studied four inches of waistline, breasts that peaked under her bra and one exposed, perfect shoulder. It was too much. "Raise your hands."

He drew the garment from her, his eyes riveted to her contoured waist. "Now the bottoms."

"Never mind. I can do it by myself," she said, shivering under his hands. "I need another hot shower. Look at me. I'm frozen."

Silky wet skin was visible on every exposed inch of her. And there were a lot of interesting areas exposed. "I know how to warm you up."

"How about my soaking in a hot bath, instead?" she answered. "I can stay in there and defrost as long as I like."

"I'll even wash your back for you," he offered as visions of Katie covered with scented bubbles floated in front of his eyes. When she turned her back to slide off the sweat-suit bottoms, he cleared his throat and admitted to himself that a gentleman would turn away. Then he grinned. When were lovers ever gentlemen?

Katie gasped. His hands were stroking her waist. At first they were merely warm and she nestled into his arms. Then his warm lips were pressing against the hollow of her throat. She turned halfway in his arms as the sweet, hot thrill of his chest met hers.

Her nipples came alive, tingled. She felt a melting hunger throb inside.

He was stroking her again. Thrills of pleasure ran down her hips. Suddenly her legs were warm as she felt his hands trail down her. Then he was still. She heard his breath drawn in. He was dropping his hand from her body.

"Oh Dak," she whispered. "Don't stop."

"I have to," he said.

But she heard the husky note in his voice. "What's wrong?"

"You wanted a bath."

"I'm all right." She tried to get back into his arms.

"You'll be better after the bath."

"You're sure of that, are you?"

"Sure I'm sure."

"Ha," she said, and drew his head to hers so she could kiss him deeply. But then he showed more strength than she could credit and turned away.

"I should make you pay for this," Katie threatened.

"That's what I'm counting on." Dak threw her a meaningful glance as he vanished into the bathroom.

He stood at the edge of the tub, pensively dropping the contents of a packet of bubble bath into the steaming-hot water. Since there had been a generous selection of powders to choose from, he'd made his own decision about which one to put into the water. Definitely not honeysuckle. This time, he intended to fulfill his fantasy.

In his mind's eye, he measured the bathtub. A tub clearly designed for the convenience and imagination of honeymooning guests. Whether or not she was willing to share it with him was another story.

Hell, he thought as he started shucking his own wet clothing, it was worth a try.

When Katie came into the bathroom wearing her terry-cloth robe, Dak was luxuriating beneath rising steam and floating mounds of bubbles.

"What in heaven's name are you doing in there?" she inquired. Her eyes widened and her lips twitched as she tried to restrain her laughter. She'd never thought to see such a virile man luxuriating in a bubble bath. Especially a male as masculine in his tastes as Dak.

"Waiting for you and thawing out in the process. I wanted to get real close to soap your back. Hurry up, the water's getting cold."

"I hate cold water," she retorted. "But it's your bath, not mine. Why don't you turn on hot water and warm it up so that it's more comfortable?"

"That's what I'm depending on you for, sweetheart. In fact, come on in. We'll warm it up that much faster."

She felt uncertain. "I never intended to bathe with you. I don't even know if it's such a good idea."

"It's one of the best I've had tonight. Come on in— I dare you."

"Not again!" Katie warned. Her uncertainty vanished. She'd never shrunk from a dare and she didn't intend to start now. "I thought you'd learned a lesson from the last time you dared me."

"Oh, I learned a lesson all right," Dak said with a rueful look on his face. "But it's one that bears repeating. Come on in."

She'd teach him a lesson in seduction he'd never forget, Katie decided as she eyed the near-to-overflowing bathtub. The temptation to show the stuff she was made of and the exotic scent of the bubble bath enticed her. "Wait a minute. I'll be back before you get a chance to miss me."

She hurried out of the bathroom and returned after she'd made a few adjustments to her appearance. Dak was leaning back against the tub with a broad smile on his face and his eyes closed. Clearly, he was anticipating *something*. But she intended to give him something more.

"Dak?"

Katie waited until he opened his eyes and sat up before she turned on her exercise tape. The throbbing, pulsing sound of a clarinet and bouzouki filled the air. The sound seemed to bring him thoroughly awake. She started to sway to the music's haunting minor key. When she had his complete attention, she wove her way around the tub, stopped in front of him and dropped her robe. Underneath, she'd draped the sheer scarves she'd worn the last time she'd played instructor.

In time to the sensuous music, she moved her hips and arms and slowly removed the scarf from her breasts. Under his avid gaze, with a flick of her wrist, she tossed it into the tub to float among the scented bubbles. Good, she mused as she saw a flush spread across his exposed torso.

Another journey around the tub brought her to Dak's right side. She salaamed, turned her back and removed the second scarf from her waist. Smiling over her shoulder, she teased him by touching him with the scarf. When his eyes widened, she dropped it over her shoulder into the water in front of him.

She heard him give a strangled laugh. "No more, please! Have mercy!"

"Not yet," she said in as sexy a voice as she could muster. "The lesson isn't over."

Gazing into his smoky eyes, Katie glided to the other side of the tub. The instruments were joined by the sound of a brush against an accompanying drum, building from sweet, soft sounds to a pulsating crescendo.

The laughter receded from his face when she reached for and unwound the third scarf from her hips, inch by transparent inch. She slowly exposed one lay of skin, then another, as his eyes widened even further in anticipation. "Has the water warmed up yet?" she asked sweetly.

Dak reared up and seized her by the waist. He pulled her into the tub and onto his lap. "Not enough," he murmured into her lips as he turned her to face him. "But I expect we'll have it sizzling in another minute or two."

As his tongue stabbed its way between her lips, Katie abandoned the rest of her plan. She could feel the hard length of him against her thighs, see the vein on his neck throbbing, hear his labored breathing.

As she melted into his arms, no doubts lingered as to how she affected him or how he touched her. She had awakened all their senses and she was more than willing to pay the price. As she sank against him and returned his embrace, the pupil became the teacher.

Chapter Thirteen

Katie gazed into Dak's sleeping face, gently touched his treasured lips with a gentle finger. He murmured in his sleep and pulled her closer. She felt warm, safe and wanted in his arms. This was the way marriage should be, she reflected with a smile. This was the perfect way to wake up in the mornings.

She gazed at the rings on the hand that rested against his warm chest. It was true he wasn't her real husband, and that he hadn't asked her to marry him. But she felt married. Nothing else could explain the happiness she felt.

The bubble bath last night had started out as a game, but laughter had soon turned into something more. A great deal more. His eyes had worshipped her; his body had joined hers, almost reverently. As if he had been afraid to break the spell that she'd created.

From the bathtub, he'd carried her to the bed. Toweled her dry before he'd joined her. His unshaven **face had rubbed her sensitive skin, but she hadn't** minded. Not when his hands had woven their magic again and again.

She'd lain in sated contentment long after he'd fallen to his side, taking her with him. She somehow sensed that their mating had been a ritual, a pledging of each other's bodies. She'd given him her body. Now she knew she'd pledged her heart to him, too. She didn't know what the morning would bring, but for now, this was enough.

She sighed and glanced at the clock. If this sojourn at the Tickle Pink Inn had been a real honeymoon, nothing could have gotten her out of bed.

It was time to make a final call to the vet, to tell him that McDuff would have to get by himself. She planned on being too occupied with her "husband."

THE SILENCE was too loud, the occasional sound of laughter too false.

When Dak guided Katie to the breakfast buffet, he immediately sensed the Toyland contingent had been infected with the fear and uncertainty of the possible theft of the blueprints.

Not only the four men and Cynthia seemed upset. Judging from the frown on Nora's face, Dak had no doubt that she was hell-bent on finding out why her usually amiable husband was pacing the floor, instead of joining her for breakfast.

Under the pretense of reaching for the orange juice, he spoke a few quiet words into Katie's ear. "There's trouble brewing at three o'clock. How about going over and diverting Nora while I get the gang together and see what I can do about solving our problem?"

Katie nodded, took her juice and moved to the table where Nora Winslow was toying with her coffee and muffins, instead of eating.

"Good morning, Nora. With all that thunder and lightning last night I could hardly manage to sleep. How about you?"

"Good morning." Nora tore her gaze away from her husband and smiled at Katie. "I was awakened a time or two, but I had Bob make me a nice hot cup of tea. That always sends me right back to sleep."

Out of the corner of her eye, Katie noticed Dak speaking to Bob Winslow and motioning to the other men and Cynthia to join them. The other wives were deep in conversation. To her dismay, the only members of the Toyland contingent missing from breakfast were Mary Lowe and Ed Mason. Hoping she was mistaken, Katie had the sinking feeling they were the topic of conversation. In an effort to distract Nora, who was bound to magnify the clandestine love affair into a major event if she heard about it, she renewed her efforts at conversation.

"How would you like to run into town today? I. Magnin has a sale. Maybe we could pick up a few souvenirs."

Nora shook her head. "No, I don't think so. Something's bothering my poor Bob. He paced the floor most of the night. As for breakfast, he says he isn't hungry. Not hungry! That man hasn't missed breakfast from the day I first married him to now. Not even when he was under the weather. No. Something is definitely wrong, and I intend to find out what it is."

"OKAY, EVERYONE, take a seat." In the boardroom, Dak waited until they had all settled down and given him their attention. "Let's get down to basics. Any ideas as to who could have gotten into the safe?"

Five silent faces stared back at him.

"All right then, to business. Now that we've all had a night to think about it, let's start at the beginning. Bob, tell me what's been going on during the meetings. Have you decided on a toy? How far along have you gotten in its development?"

Winslow glanced around the table as if seeking a consensus before he started speaking. Four heads nodded as one, although Dak could see a great deal of reluctance in the conferee's eyes.

"Well, back at Toyland," Winslow said in measured tones, "we tossed ideas around and decided that the hottest toys on the market today were action figures. Once marketing defined the product, and based on surveys made before we got here, we've come up with an idea that seems promising. It's some sort of an action creature from another planet. We code-named it Planetarians. Hal made some schematics and Cynthia some preliminary drawings. We've been playing around with the idea and it was looking good."

It *was* looking good? Dak refused to believe the party was over. "What do you do with the blueprints and the freehand drawings at the end of a session?"

"Count every blasted one of them before we put them in the safe. In the morning, at the start of each session, we count them again. We weren't going to let anything get by us. At least," he said, running his hand across his sweating forehead, "we thought nothing was getting by us."

"Well, according to Dak, it looks as if something has, doesn't it?" Hal Martin said bitterly. "We're dead meat."

"Wait a minute!" Dak interrupted. "You said you count each drawing every night and tally them up again in the morning?"

"Yes." Bob glanced around the table. "Right?" The others nodded. "Hell, Dak, you ought to know. You're the one who locks the safe and opens it every morning."

Five pairs of eyes fixed on Dak.

"I hadn't realized you counted them twice a day, although it's a damn good idea," Dak replied. "Do you make copies?"

"No. But if we did, they'd be in the safe, too."

Dak met Bob Winslow's accusing stare head-on. Since he and Katie had the only keys to the boardroom and he was the only one with the combination to the safe, it was looking more and more as if they were moving to the head of the list of suspects. He had to do something drastic before Gibson was called in. Katie's idea of searching every suite was sounding better and better every minute. All he needed was to clear the decks for action. "There's obviously more to this than a simple theft."

"There's nothing simple about it! Especially since all the drawings and blueprints are accounted for. All we have to go on is your say-so that some were stolen." Bob Winslow jumped to his feet and glared at Dak across the conference table. "You're the head of Toyland's security. What are you going to do about it?"

"Tell you what," Dak said after a few moments of deep thought. "Your wives are getting pretty edgy about your disappearing every day when you've supposedly taken them on a second honeymoon. You, too, Cynthia. Ed's been acting pretty bored, too."

"Bored? Hardly," she answered bitterly. "He's perked up since he—"

"Give it a rest, Cynthia. We're not here to discuss Ed." At the watchful look that came over Richard Lowe's face, Dak rushed to stop Cynthia from broadcasting her husband's interest in Mary. There was trouble enough without adding a sexual triangle to their problems.

"Or Katie?"

"What about Katie?" Dak's eyes narrowed. His charitable feelings about Cynthia dissipated. As far as he was concerned, she was the hellion she'd appeared to be, after all.

"Strange that she turns up here with two husbands. We know who you are, but who's this Steve Dana?"

"There's a reasonable explanation. Not that Katie owes you one. It has nothing to do with the subject at hand."

"It might have everything to do with the subject at hand," Richard Lowe broke in. "Sounds to me as if you're prejudiced in favor of your wife."

Dak's sympathy for the guy evaporated. "Tell you what," he finally managed when he'd counted to ten. "I imagine everyone could use a little time off to relieve the stress we've been under this week." He was rewarded by an assenting chorus. "Let's see if we can rent a yacht up in Monterey. You can all go for a cruise with your spouses. I'll stay behind and see what I can do around here to figure things out. Maybe, if I have the place to myself, I can find out what's going on."

"Now you're talking!" Winslow strode to the door. "Nora's going to have my hide if I don't start paying attention to her sometime soon. I'm not even certain she's bought the golfing and the fishing bit. Fact is, I'm as lazy as hell, and Nora knows it. A cruise ought to do the trick."

"Me, too," Hal added. "It would go a long way to getting me out of the doghouse."

In quick order, everyone rushed out the door. This time, to Dak's relief, the laughter was genuine. He checked the meeting room, locked the door and followed Winslow.

"AND NOW WHAT?" Katie asked as the inn's pink van finally vanished down the road, delayed by the late appearances of Ed and Mary. "Thank goodness they showed up separately and acted as if nothing happened."

"We start searching." He glanced at Steve Dana. "Come on down to the terrace, where we can get some privacy, and I'll fill you in on what's going on. That is, if you want to get involved."

"Anything to get this gig over with." Dana threw him a wry look. "From the weird things that have been happening around here, I don't think anyone could have written a script like this one if they'd tried. I ought to know—I've played a lot of 'em."

"You haven't heard or seen anything yet," Dak assured him. "You may change your mind when you know the whole story."

After Dak explained the situation and the problem of the possible missing documents, Steve roared with laughter. "You were right. I *haven't* seen or heard anything like this scenario. But, as long as I'm here and able to help out, just what is it you want me to do?''

"Katie and I are going to search everyone's rooms. We'd like you to act as a lookout. If you see anyone coming, or if you see anything out of the ordinary going on, knock on the door."

"Got it. Say, just out of curiosity, what are you going to use for a key?"

"I've explained the problem of the possible missing prints to Mrs. Fraser," Dak replied, glancing over at Katie to see her reaction. She didn't fail him. Her expression spoke eloquently of what she thought of the Dakota Smith Fan Club. He shrugged. A guy had to do what a guy had to do. "She said it would be okay if she came along to make certain we didn't disturb anything."

"Good Lord, that's all we need! Mrs. Fraser dogging our footsteps and wondering about Steve and me," Katie grumbled as she consulted her notes. "Now that we've eliminated Ed Mason, where shall we start? Hal Martin?"

"Right. Just give me a few minutes to round up our chaperon." Dak took off for the office.

"You didn't tell the Harington Agency about any of this when you signed up and got me, did you?"

"That's because I didn't know Dak was going to be one step ahead of me. Or that there would be a theft."

"Just got lucky, eh?"

Katie gazed off to where Dak had disappeared. She thought about how much he had changed from the bitter, resentful man she'd first met in Gibson's office. This Dak was tender, thoughtful, caring. A man who seemed to understand the part of her that marched to a different drummer. A man who could even understand her talking to a sea otter and not think she'd lost her mind. A man who held her in his arms and made her feel precious. Lucky? Definitely.

"You could say so," she finally replied, hoping that the dreamy feeling spreading through her wasn't obvious.

"I definitely do." Steve grinned. "You've fallen for Dak like a ton of bricks."

"Is it that obvious?"

"You bet. Lucky guy."

Dak returned with Mrs. Fraser in tow. From her uneasy glances, Katie could tell the woman's heart wasn't in it.

"Now remember," Mrs. Fraser said as she opened the door to the Martin suite, "you're to look, but not to touch anything. If you see something out of the way, tell me. I'll decide if we can examine it more closely."

"Don't worry," Dak reassured her. "We won't take but a few minutes. Blueprints ought to be easy enough to spot."

"I wouldn't be doing this at all if it weren't for the inn's reputation," she answered as she led the way inside the suite. "We can't afford to have any rumors going around. This is a respectable establishment."

With Mrs. Fraser dogging her footsteps, ten minutes later Katie shook her head. "There's no sign of blueprints. Unless we open suitcases?"

Mrs. Fraser gasped. "Definitely not!"

"Then I guess we'll have to move on." Katie cast a last look around the suite as she left.

"Next?" Dak peered over her shoulder.

"Moriarity. He seems too innocent. You said that kind needs to be watched. Remember?"

"Yeah, I remember. But..." His voice trailed off into an exasperated sigh.

Katie patted his hand in sympathy as they moved next door. She was getting frustrated, too. She was pretty confident that unless Mrs. F. relented, checking this room—or any other, for that matter—was going to have the same barren result. She paused to consider her next move. What if she got Steve to engage the manager in a conversation about TV soaps? Was the move covered by the detective's code of ethics?

"Katie, wait up a minute." Dak steered her away from the door to the Moriarity suite. "You've got something on your mind. I can tell by the way your eyes lit up. Give."

"Oh," she whispered behind her hand. "I was just wondering if we could get Steve to divert Mrs. F. while we do some thorough searching. We'll never get anywhere this way. Of course," she added quietly, "if it's against the law, I'll forget it."

"Sweetheart, there's another saying in the security business. It's okay to bend the rules if the end justifies the means."

They exchanged conspiratorial glances. Katie slowly nodded. "I like that one a lot. Did you make it up, or is for real?"

Dak didn't dare tell her he learned the adage at his wily old grandfather's knee, or that he applied it whenever it became necessary or just convenient.

He was prepared to burn if it made her happy. Or if it solved the mystery of the riffled safe. Besides, Dak had the idea that if Katie liked an idea, it had to be a good one. Ethics or morals be damned. Good, he thought as he grinned down at her. She was his kind of operative.

"I'm going to talk to Steve while you go inside with Mrs. F."

TWO SUITES LATER, the results were the same. Nothing. With or without Mrs. Fraser.

"Any more good ideas?" Dak asked after he'd thanked the manager and trailed back to the terrace, where the wine-and-cheese happy hour was about to take place. After today's empty showing, he needed a cool glass of wine. "It's today or never. Once everyone gets back, we won't have a chance like this again."

"You didn't cover everyone on Katie's list," Steve offered. "We only checked three suites."

"I hardly think Bob Winslow would have done it. He's the team leader," Katie mused as she studied her notes.

"How about that guy Ed Mason and his wife?"

"Looks like all he was after was a one-night stand. We crossed him off the list," Dak announced as he paced the terrace. "Damn! I wish I knew where to go from here."

"Seems to me that all you've talked about is Mason. What about his wife?"

Dak stopped in his tracks to stare at Steve. "What about his wife?"

"From the way you described the conference, she was on the scene of the crime, wasn't she?"

Katie and Dak looked at each other. "By George, he's right!" Dak exclaimed. "We've completely forgotten Cynthia! I'm going to get Mrs. F. back here."

"You may not have to," Steve said pensively. "When we left the hall, I saw housekeeping's cleaning wagon parked outside a door. Maybe you could persuade the maid to let one of you in."

"Katie?"

She hesitated only briefly. She couldn't stand to see the anxiety in Dak's eyes. Hated to think that he—or the both of them, for that matter—would have to bear the brunt of accusations they had no way to refute, and that their jobs were at stake. It wasn't herself she was worried about so much. It was Dak. For him, she was ready to do anything.

"Okay," she said bravely. "I'll meet you guys back here as soon as I can. Save me a glass of wine. Oh, and some of those chocolate-chip cookies they serve."

"You can't eat chocolate," Dak admonished, remembering she was a graduate of Chocoholics Anonymous.

"Just one as a reward," she said as she turned away, "After this, I feel I owe myself something special."

"No way," he called after her. "I can think of another reward you'll like a whole better."

"You're right." She smiled at him over her shoulder as she disappeared. **"Hold on to that thought."**

Steve's eyebrows rose as he listened to the verbal exchange. "From the story you told me about how and why you came up here pretending to be Katie's husband, I used to think you two were enemies."

"Not anymore," Dak assured him. "Not since I've had a chance to learn more about that redhead and about myself, too."

WHEN KATIE reached the Masons' suite, the maid was nowhere in sight. Hesitating only for a moment, she glanced cautiously around the hall and quietly stepped through the open door. The suite had already been serviced and everything looked neat and tidy. Remembering her earlier promise to Mrs. Fraser not to disturb any private belongings, she checked the desk drawers, glanced into the closets and searched the shelves before moving on to the bedroom.

Frustrated because she couldn't open any dresser drawers, she checked the room and under the bed. She came up empty. A cursory check of the bathroom left her more upset than ever. If there were any blueprints or drawings around, they weren't obvious. The closed suitcases on a stand were tempting, but they were off-limits.

Katie knew she had to move fast before anyone came back to the suite. After a last quick glance around, she started to leave. Suddenly her unfailingly reliable sixth sense vibrated. She stopped in her tracks and glanced back at the closet door. Ed Mason's raincoat, neatly hung on the open closet door, signaled her as surely as a red flag.

WHEN KATIE reappeared looking wide-eyed, Dak knew she'd hit pay dirt. He nudged Steve away from the crackers-and-cheese tray and they went to meet her.

To Dak's astonishment, Katie rose on tiptoe and planted a big kiss at the side of Steve's lips. "What's that all about?" Dak growled. Damn, he thought, only half-amused.

"Steve deserves a reward, too," Katie said. "He saw something we overlooked and he turned out to be absolutely right!"

"You found something in the Masons' suite?" Dak edged Katie away from Steve and marched her to a quiet corner. Steve glanced at the other guests who were gathering for the wine-and-cheese reception and followed.

"Yes, I did. Reduced photocopies of blueprints!"

"Photocopies? You're sure?"

"Of course I am. I put them in our room for safekeeping."

"Good." Dak wanted to ravish her... but in a less public place. If what she had found were actually blueprints and sketches of the proposed toy, they were finally off the hot seat. "Where did you find them?"

"Believe it or not, in an inner pocket of Ed Mason's raincoat where it was hanging in the closet. I figured a suitcase or a drawer was too obvious a place to hide it. Besides, I wanted to keep my word to Mrs. Fraser that I wouldn't open anything unless she was there."

"So he *had* gotten into the boardroom when you saw him prowling around at midnight!"

"Yes. And that's not all. There were a couple of Cynthia's sketches in there, too."

They traded thoughtful glances. Steve was the first to speak.

"I may not know a hell of a lot about the way criminal minds work, but don't you think leaving the prints and sketches in such an open place was a little too pat?"

Dak nodded slowly. Too pat, and maybe even an invitation. "Steve's right. Something about this isn't kosher. And I intend to find out what it is before the day is through." He grinned at Steve. "Anytime you get tired of acting, let me know. I'd be proud to have you join my staff."

"No, thanks." Steve shook his head. "I didn't do anything special. Fact is, sometimes you can get so involved in trying to solve a problem you can't see the answer staring you in the face. It takes an outsider to see the obvious. As for me, I'm an actor at heart. And after this job as Katie's hired husband, I'm going to work harder at trying to get on the stage. Maybe even give up the soaps. Well, if you don't need me anymore, I think I'll go and clean up. Ellen will be back pretty soon. I promised to take her out to dinner up at Moss Landing."

"Thanks. We sure appreciate everything." Dak shook hands with Steve.

Ignoring Dak's frown, Katie hugged Steve again. "Thank you so much. You've turned out to be a good friend."

"Even if I didn't make it as your husband?" Steve laughingly replied with one eye on Dak. "Somehow I doubt you'll need to hire a husband again. If you need me for anything else, don't hesitate to call." He hugged Katie back, clapped Dak on the shoulder and started to leave. "I don't expect I'll be the target of any more midnight visits, right?"

"Right," Dak said firmly, his arm around Katie's waist. "Not a chance."

"Let's go look at the stuff you found," Dak added when Steve had gone. "If it's what I think it is, Cynthia and Ed owe Toyland an explanation."

Chapter Fourteen

Steve's warning echoed in his mind. Katie's find appeared to be everything Dak needed to confirm his belief. The safe had been tampered with. He stared at the four reduced-size blueprints, examined the freehand sketches lying on the coffee table. He should have been elated. He wasn't.

"I thought you'd be pleased," Katie said, frowning over his silence. "Is there something wrong?"

"You might say so." He paced the floor, stopping to glance down at the small stack of papers spread out on the table. "I keep remembering that the team insisted there were no blueprints missing."

"And?"

"So how come you were able to find these?"

"Beats me." Katie shrugged as she bent over to examine the papers. "If there's something wrong with them, I sure can't tell what it is. Say, will you look at this drawing! The colors are so vivid you would think it was an original."

"Hold up a minute!" Dak stopped his pacing and strode back to the table. He picked up a blueprint, reached for the drawing and held them both to the light. "The drawing is an original—I'm positive," he said as he examined it. "The blueprint is another story. It's obviously a copy. See the faint fingerprints here in the corner? They never would have shown up so prominently if this was the original."

Katie leaned forward and compared the drawings and the blueprints. Dak was obviously right. She never would have figured it out by herself. "Now where does that leave us?"

"I'm afraid it means that someone copied the blueprints before the originals were placed in the safe," he reasoned. "And in order to mislead us, turned the combination lock to make it look as if it had been opened. That's why the count of what was put in the safe at night and taken out in the mornings was never off. As for these drawings, if they're originals, it means they could have been made anytime."

"And put in the pocket of Ed's raincoat? Who would want to do something like that?"

"Well, Madam Detective, I'd say it would take an artist . . . who was able to make copies of the original blueprints. And one who could make the copies even after the official drawings were put in the safe. The perpetrator seems pretty obvious to me," Dak suggested to a shocked Katie. "How about to you?"

"Cynthia Mason! No, she couldn't have."

"Bingo! Come on, we have some planning to do. In my book, Cynthia has a great deal of explaining to do when she gets back."

"YOU AND KATIE should have come along with us. We sailed down the coast, did a little fishing, had a picnic lunch aboard and even a happy hour on the way back!'' Bob Winslow, his arm around his Nora, beamed at Dak. ''The little woman here sure enjoyed herself. Didn't you, Pudding Pie?''

''Bob, watch your language!'' Nora poked her husband with her elbow. ''We're in public. The whole world doesn't need to know our secrets.''

Winslow grinned broadly and wrapped an arm around his wife's ample waist. ''I call her my Pudding Pie because she feels silky like a pudding and because apple pie is her favorite dessert. And she's my favorite dessert!''

''Oh my goodness!'' Nora covered her crimson face with her hands and rushed from the foyer.

Dak reluctantly swallowed his laughter. He hated to dampen Winslow's spirits, but it had to be done. He took him aside. ''I think Katie and I have solved our problem. We may even have found the culprit.''

Winslow sobered and lowered his voice. ''You're sure?''

''I'm sure.''

''Hell!'' The jocular man seemed to age before Dak's eyes. His ruddy complexion turned white; worry lines appeared on his forehead; his normally laughing eyes turned bleak. ''I was so positive nothing was missing, that you were wrong. I was willing to stake my job on it!''

''You won't have to,'' Dak reassured him. ''If you have time before going on to dinner, I'd like to have the group convene in the boardroom. I'll lay it out for all of you.''

''Tell me first! I don't like being kept in the dark.''

''I'd rather not. You'll see why if you give me an hour.''

"To hell with dinner! Let me go round up the team and meet you downstairs. Give me ten minutes."

"I'll get Katie and meet you there."

"You sure you want to involve Katie?" Winslow frowned and looked around him. "Considering what's at stake, the fewer people who know about this, the better."

"Sorry. Whether you intended to or not, you've just as much as accused me and my wife of having something to do with this mess," Dak said quietly. "She's entitled to be there while she and I clear ourselves."

My wife! Dak was surprised to hear the word roll off his tongue as naturally as if Katie had been his all along. Considering the way he'd felt about marriage before he'd met her just a few weeks ago, the revelation startled and pleased him.

The fact was, in the few short days they'd been together, he *had* begun to think of her as his wife. And to have developed a fierce protective feeling for the clever redhead. No matter how independent and capable she might be, there was something about her that fueled a need to watch out for her. What had started as a physical union of their bodies had wound up being a connecting of their minds.

Dak had the feeling that Katie was many women wrapped up in one surprise package. He looked forward to unwrapping each one.

Determined not to let her out of his sight until the "coming out party" was over, he excused himself and went to get her and the evidence that would clear them.

She was waiting for him in the suite, a shopping bag in hand.

"This is no time to think of going shopping," he told her. "I've made arrangements for the team to meet us in the boardroom right away,"

"Just like a man." Katie smiled to soften her reply. "I had no intention of going shopping tonight. But—" she paused to let her words sink in "—I had every intention of putting the evidence where no one could possibly imagine it was there. Everyone is so used to seeing women carrying shopping bags, no one would ever think there's serious stuff in here."

"Katie, Katie, you are a wonder," Dak said fondly, reaching for her and nuzzling her scented hair. He had a feeling that he might never fully discover all that was uniquely her, no matter how long and well they would get to know each other. He enveloped her in his arms, shopping bag and all. He kissed her eyebrows, her nose, her chin and finally wound up nibbling at her lips. "What's the name of that detective school you graduated from?"

"I never said I graduated from a detective school. That was your idea," she managed in between kisses. She knew she'd passed some sort of a test, that he no longer resented her coming up with ideas. He accepted her as a full partner and even welcomed her help. She couldn't remember ever being so happy. "Why would you want to know, anyway?"

"I want to sign up for a postgraduate course," he said. "Seems as if there are still a few things I need to learn." When she returned his kiss with a passion that shook him from the top of his head to his size-thirteen feet, he knew they'd crossed some invisible line.

Breathless, Katie could only stare at him when he finally held her away from him to admire her. Her

fingers trembled as she touched her lips. Dak had held
and kissed her with a fierceness, as if they'd never
shared a kiss before and might never again. It was almost as though they hadn't shared two magic-filled
nights. As though he couldn't wait for another.

She couldn't wait, either, she realized as she moved
back into the warmth of his welcoming arms. No
matter how much he'd loved her, she wanted, needed
more. Needed the reassurance that he saw her for what
she was: not a competitor, but an independent person, though a woman nevertheless. She ached to have
him make love to her again, feel heated skin against
heated skin, see his eyes grow stormy with the passion
that echoed her own. To be swept away again into another world in his arms.

Although all of his lovemaking had been memora-
ble, this kiss had somehow been different, she thought
with another rise of passion. There had been an intensity in the eyes that had caressed her as surely as his
arms and his lips had enveloped her. The kiss had been
more than just a passion; it had been a commitment.
It had been a beginning to build a dream on.

"Katie, I—"

She put her fingers across his lips. "Don't say anything now. Remember, first things first. We have a job
to accomplish."

DAK REMOVED the picture that covered the wall safe
while Katie spread the papers she'd found in Ed Mason's raincoat across the table.

"Come over here." Dak held out his hand to Katie.
"I'd like you to stand beside me while we spring the
trap. You're just as much responsible for solving this

puzzle as I am. Maybe more." He wrapped his hand around hers. Katie was the perfect partner. They understood and picked up on each other's thoughts. He hoped she was on the same wavelength as he was right now. "This won't take too long," he assured her. "And then . . ."

She dimpled and nodded. "You're next on my list of unfinished business, too, Mr. Smith."

"This had better be good," Hal spouted angrily as he stalked through the door. "Bob practically grabbed me out of the shower and insisted I show up here right away."

"Me, too," Pat griped behind his back. "Molly is madder than hell at my having to disappear so suddenly."

"Mary's not so happy, either." Richard Lowe glowered at Dak. "I got the distinct feeling that she's not too happy about the whole blasted so-called second honeymoon. I *know* it's because I've had to leave her alone too often and too long. And you're not helping one bit!"

"Come on, Richard. If you've had any marital problems on this trip, they must have started long before now." Dak motioned at the table. "Take a look at these."

Everyone edged closer to the table. Bob glanced at the drawings and over at the wall to where the landscape had been removed to reveal the safe. "You just take those out of the safe?"

"No. And to prove it, I'm going to open the safe while you watch. I'll want you to count the number of drawings and blueprints to verify that the number is the same as the last time you counted them."

Dak could feel eyes boring into his back as he opened the wall safe and withdrew its contents. He motioned Winslow forward, handed the package to him, then stood aside as the man counted and recounted the blueprints and drawings.

"Everything's here, all right!" Winslow threw them on the table. "Now what?"

One by one, Dak caught the gaze of each of the other conferees. Richard Lowe colored, but Dak knew the man's embarrassment had nothing to do with the possible theft of the blueprints. The poor guy obviously remembered Dak's last remark about Lowe's unhappy marriage. The way he gazed around him defiantly, he probably sensed that everyone knew about Mary's involvement with Ed Mason.

Pat and Hal had calmed down and were comparing the duplicate blueprints and drawings with the originals. After a long, thoughtful moment, Dak wrote the men off. They appeared too puzzled to be guilty. That left only Cynthia Mason. As far as Dak was concerned, she looked—and was—as guilty as hell.

"There's only one person who could have rendered duplicate drawings," he announced quietly. "And that person also could easily have copied a few blueprints to make it appear as if there had been a theft . . . when there hadn't been one at all."

"But the safe—didn't you say the dial had been tampered with?" Winslow frowned at the safe, picked up a drawing and blueprint from the ones Dak had removed and studied them closely one more time. "You're right. Both of the drawings are originals. What are you driving at?"

"The dial had merely been turned to make it seem as if someone had gotten into the safe." Dak's gaze lingered on the culprit. "Am I right, Cynthia?"

All eyes focused on Cynthia Mason.

"You planted the papers, didn't you, Cynthia?" Dak added quietly. "You wanted the drawings to be found."

After a short silence, Cynthia spoke up, defiance evident in every line of her body and in her every word. "Why are you so sure I did it? How do you know Ed didn't leave them in his raincoat himself?"

"I didn't remember mentioning finding them in your husband's raincoat. You did," Dak said into the silence. He steeled himself to deal the final blow. "And I'm so sure because you're the only one who could have drawn the toy exactly as it appears in the drawings in the safe." He watched the guilt flood her face. It gave him no pleasure.

Not so long ago, Dak realized, this revelation would have deepened his distrust in women. Thank God, he thought with a loving glance at Katie, he'd finally found a woman he could trust. He was willing to bet there wasn't a deceitful bone in Katie's delectable body.

She must have sensed the way he felt. She smiled at him before she turned her attention back to Cynthia.

"Why would you do a thing like this?" Winslow burst out as he surged to his feet. "Why?"

"You needn't explain right now." Katie let go of Dak's hand and moved to Cynthia's side. She'd suddenly realized why she clung to a husband like Ed Mason: she loved the man, even as she hated him. Love and hate were two very powerful emotions.

Given the same circumstances, Katie wondered how far she would go if she were in the same situation. She glanced back at Dak, read the love and concern in his eyes. He was a decent and honorable man, he would never treat her as Ed Mason had treated his wife. She felt the same way. She could never hurt the man she loved.

"The only ones who need to know the answer are Dak and Neil Gibson," Katie told Cynthia as she put her arm around the stricken woman's shoulder. "But in the long run, it wasn't worth it, was it?"

"No," Cynthia said quietly as she raised her head to gaze at the puzzled faces around her. Tears flowed from the corners of her eyes. "No. I've known all along Ed wasn't worth it. But he was mine, with all his faults. I couldn't help loving him just the same. Evidently he didn't feel that way about me. I was jealous of his attention to Mary. I'd hoped he would look on this trip as a second honeymoon, that we could reconcile our differences. It just finally got to be too much for me to take. I wanted to punish him by making it appear he was a thief."

She turned to face the others. "I apologize for the problems I've caused," she said bravely, "but I want you all to know that these papers didn't leave the premises. I haven't told anyone a thing about the new toy. You have my promise that I won't."

Winslow nodded. "Thank you for that. But I will expect to have your letter of resignation before you and Ed leave the inn."

"SORRY I TOOK so long," Dak called as he came into the suite. "I had to close up shop." He found Katie on the patio, staring off into the distance. The setting sun had painted the horizon with vivid colors of orange and red against the blue-and-gray sky. The dejected way she leaned against the railing told him that the afternoon's triumph had held no particular joy for her. Any more than it had for him.

Dak was sorry for Richard and Mary Lowe. He felt a sadness for what he realized must surely be the end of their marriage. And for Cynthia, who had loved unwisely. But he also felt relieved that this triangle of misunderstandings was sorting itself out. He'd found Katie in the midst of all this. His life, which had once seemed so empty, now focused on this slender woman with the wild wind-tossed hair and the fiery nature to match.

His Katie was a unique woman. If falling in love was an act of the imagination for some people, his growing affection for her was real. If he read her correctly, she felt the same way. Other marriages might be ending, but his real one to Katie might just be beginning. They may have put the cart before the horse by honeymooning first, but there was still time to remedy that. He was going to take care of it before another night was over.

Katie was lost in thought. She felt the warmth of his body next to her, but she didn't stir when he came up behind her. He put his arms around her and buried his face in her fragrant hair. She smelled of sweet honeysuckle blossoms, and something else he couldn't quite place.

She turned into his arms. "I'm glad this day is over."

"So am I," Dak replied, as he held her closely. "And for the same reason, sweetheart. It's never easy to watch other people's misfortune, is it?"

She shook her head. "No, it isn't. There's not much satisfaction in being right, is there?"

"No." Dak hated to see her so unhappy. It was time to turn their thoughts to something else. He hugged her, kissed the sides of each of her luminous eyes, her lips. And discovered a way to put a smile on her face.

"Be careful now," he teased. "If I thought you were a woman who'd let a guy be right once in a while, I just might have to propose, and where would I be?"

"So that's what's on your mind, is it?" She glanced at him through long lashes.

"Katie, you've been eating chocolate, haven't you?" he teased. "And after you swore you were a graduate of Chocoholics Anonymous!"

"Cookies," she said. "After a day like this, I felt I owed myself a special treat."

"But..."

"I know, I know. But food sometimes is a special reward. Maybe I shouldn't have eaten those cookies," she said, laughing. "I guess I haven't been able to give up all my old habits."

"Really?" Dak regarded her with speculation. "What other bad habits do you have that I don't know about?"

Katie knew, from the devilish look in Dak's eyes, he had something in particular on his mind. "Nothing, really. Nothing as bad as this one."

"How about your exotic dancing, or do you call it merely exercise?"

"Dancing?" She felt herself color. "What do you know about my dancing?"

"Exotic dancing," he corrected.

Katie thought quickly. Somehow he had found out she'd paid her way through college by working as a belly dancer. When had he seen her dancing? The answer came as she recalled his saying "exercise."

"You watched me exercise?" she demanded. The thought embarrassed her. The only time she'd taken the time to exercise had been just before she showered each morning. "What else did you see?"

"Not a thing, I swear." Dak backed away from her ire. "On my honor."

Still not completely mollified, Katie sniffed. "Next time, knock."

"Next time, Katie," he said as he ran his finger down her cheek and down her neck, "you just might costume up and let me see the real thing."

She felt herself color as she envisioned herself wearing little more than strings of beads and undulating in front of him. To lessen the tension, she had to make a joke of it "Don't be silly. Belly dancing is a form of seduction, a theatrical act intended to be performed in front of an audience."

"I'm perfectly willing to be an audience of one," Dak answered. "Try me...I dare you." He left her standing in the patio and sauntered back to the couch. "I'm ready when you are."

Why not? thought Katie. He'd dared her once too often. This time she'd call his bluff. Too bad she didn't have one of her costumes with her. Still, she was determined to do it in style. And burn him to a cinder in the process.

"Pour yourself a drink while I change," she offered as she passed him on the way to the bedroom. "I won't be long."

"No, thanks. I want to be fully alert for this one." He leaned against the pillows, stretched out his long legs. "Take your time. I've got all night."

MUSIC? Dak wondered if his imagination was doing a number on him. The Greek song "Misralou" sounded through the slatted sliding doors, its minor key bringing with it visions of an Arabian marketplace, a Turkish harem. Moments later, the doors slid open. A hand appeared; a bare leg slid down the door frame; a bare shoulder beckoned to him. He swallowed hard and fought his reaction. It was only the start of the show and he was practically seduced already.

Then Katie floated into the room in a swirl of silk and bowed before him. Her eyes were outlined with kohl, eyelashes darkened with mascara, her eyelids colored with green eye shadow. Her cheeks glowed with shades of pink rouge. Her lips shone a vivid red under a sheer scarf that covered her face from her eyes to below her chin. Long, tinkling silver earrings hung from her ears. Her auburn hair, interwoven with a string of pearls, hung loose.

Mesmerized by the exotic vision moving slowly toward him, he let his fascinated gaze move lower.

She was wearing the exotic bridal negligee from Victoria's Secret. From what he could glimpse, underneath the robe there were a few strategically placed sheer scarfs.

He'd once vowed to burn for Katie if he'd had to, Dak thought as he sat up and gave her his undivided attention. Now he was on fire because of her. He didn't know how much more of this he could take.

She launched into alluring undulations. In slow motion, she pointed her toes, extended her legs one by one, moved her hips from side to side. Her movements brought her directly in front of him. In time to the music, she undid the top ribbons that tied the negligee together, leaving only the one at her waist. She turned her back to him, and, arms waving in the air, swayed from side to side. When her rib cage and shoulders moved in opposition to her hips, creating a sinuous motion, Dak rose to his feet and made for the ice bucket.

"Had enough?" Katie inquired sweetly. She'd seen that look often enough to know the effect her dance was having on him. But a dare was a dare. He'd brought it upon himself.

Earrings tinkled in her wake as she closed her eyes, executed to a figure eight with her hips and followed in his footsteps. When she gave him a practiced seductive smile and stopped inches away from him, she could feel his body heat. His eyes appeared glazed as he turned to face her, a forgotten glass of ice water in his hand. He'll think twice about daring me again, she decided happily as she wound her way around him. When the tape ended, she extended her hands in front of her and bowed low in the salaam she'd learned at dancing school.

"Had enough?" she asked again.

There was a bemused look on Dak's face as he took her by her shoulders and raised her to face him. "More than enough. I think you'd better quit while I'm ahead."

He stopped her as she nodded graciously and turned away toward the bedroom. "Not without me, you don't," he said as he swung her into his arms. "Not after this."

"The first thing I want to do is to make it clear that your dancing has nothing to do with what I'm going to say," he stated as he made his way back to the couch. "And I think it would be better said out here.

"Of course," he continued, as he sank into the cushions with Katie in his lap and drew the veil from her face, "this lovely seduction of yours is just icing on the cake. Look at me, sweetheart. What I wanted to tell you is that I love you. I think I started falling in love with you the first time I saw you dressed in those ridiculous blue sweats, ready to do battle. And I was finally hooked when you threatened to feed me to that little sea otter."

Katie's heart melted as she saw the truth in his gaze, but she was almost afraid to believe him. "You once said I was all the things you disliked in a woman."

"Maybe what I should have said is that you make me see all the things I dislike about myself," he said, kissing her ring finger. "I admit I was afraid of making another mistake, but I began to admire you more and more every day." He shrugged as he outlined her lips with a gentle touch. "I love the way your mind works, those wise sayings of yours. Even when you've driven me to distraction with worry over you. I'm gambling that you love me, too."

"Oh, I do. I do," Katie answered. "It's just that I never knew how you were feeling. I thought that not sleeping on the couch was all you cared about."

"Oh, I care about sleeping in the bed, all right, but not enough to make love to you to get it. Marry me, Katie. And if that's what it will take to prove to you that I love you for yourself, I'll even sleep out here on the couch until you say yes."

"That won't be necessary," Katie whispered, her heart so full of love she could hardly bear it. "When did you have in mind?"

"As soon as I can get a special license so we can get married up here."

"Oh, how perfect. I can't think of a more romantic place to get married, but I don't think it would be wise. Everyone will know I've never been married to either you or Steve."

"I'm pretty sure no one thinks you're married to Steve after today, but if that bothers you, we'll fly up to Reno over the weekend to get married. No one ever need know the truth."

She started to undo the last tie at her waist. "I like that idea better. In the meantime..."

Katie slid from Dak's lap, letting her negligee fall to the floor. "I'll get dressed so we can go to dinner. Funny thing, though," she said as she glanced back at him, "I don't seem to be very hungry tonight. How about you?"

"I know another wise saying," Dak said as he followed her into the bedroom. "'Man does not live by bread alone.'"

"Or cookies," Katie said, smiling an invitation over her shoulder.

"There's no use wasting a perfectly good honeymoon, is there?" he asked. He unwound the scarves she'd tied over her and ran his hands over her glistening body. She was everything a man could want in a woman, and not only for this, he thought as he kissed his way to her lips.

Who cared in which order love, marriage and a honeymoon came, as long as they came with the man she wanted, needed? Katie thought as she watched Dak undress. Or that a sea otter could play matchmaker? When Dak lifted her onto the bed and covered her with his own throbbing body, she stopped questioning how and why they'd found each other and kissed him with all the passion in her.

Sparkling diamonds burst behind her closed eyes when he brought her to the culmination of her dreams. They'd become equals in life and in love. That was all that mattered. What had begun as a desperate masquerade had become true.

"I love you," he whispered into her ear. "I know it will always be this way."

"It will be. We'll never disagree again," she said.

As Dak gazed at his feisty Katie, he smiled inwardly. "I wouldn't bet on it."

Epilogue

"Hi, Rachel, this is Katie O'Connor. Sorry I missed you, but I wanted to tell you that I got married—no, not to Steve Dana, but to Dakota Smith. Yes, I know I said I was avoiding him, but now we make love, not war. Next spring, we're expecting our first child. If it's a boy, his name will be Justin—"

"No, Katie, I thought it was going to be Nicholas," a voice cut in.

"Well, I've changed my mind. Besides, you said you didn't like Dak Junior."

"I don't. By the way, whatever happened to 'Mac'?"

"It sounds like a truck!"

"Katie..."

"Rachel, I'll call you back."

And there are more husbands!
Turn the page for a bonus look at what's in
store for you in the next *1-800-HUSBAND*
book. It's a sneak preview of

THE LAST BRIDESMAID
by Leandra Logan
October 1995

*"Whether you want him for business ... or
pleasure, for one month or one night, we have
the husband you've been looking for. When
circumstances dictate the appearance of a man
in your life, call 1-800-HUSBAND for an
uncomplicated, uncompromising solution.
Call now. Operators standing by...."*

Don't miss
#601 THE LAST BRIDESMAID
by Leandra Logan!

Chapter One

"Need a man in your life?"

Jill's spine stiffened as the husky radio voice filled the quiet hollow of the property room. It was as if the voice were speaking directly to her. Thankfully, the desk clerk was behind her and couldn't see her expression.

"Are you a happily single businesswoman who occasionally needs a partner? An unattached female who is weary of scrambling for a last-minute escort? If so, the Harrington Agency would like to help. Let one of our husbands act as your other half. Dial 1-800-HUSBAND now. The lines are open twenty-four hours a day."

Jill remained stock-still as the commercial faded away and the "Doctor Love" radio program took over the airwaves again.

"Bunch of hooey, isn't it?" Mel Clooney said. "All my wives managed to find a man in me, didn't they?"

Yeah, and all your ex-wives are as single as I am. "Not everyone is as lucky as your women," she returned sweetly. "Let me outta here, will you?" Hugging her clipboard close to her chest, she retreated to the detective room.

But there on her desk was a picture of her with her four high school cronies, Penny, Gayle, Rebecca and

Alison. They were like family—and now, with Penny's engagement, they would all be married. All except her.

Before graduation, they'd predicted Jill would be the first to marry. To Roger Bannon, her steady. That was until the breakup....

Jill was trapped. She couldn't say no to Penny's wedding. But how could she go back home and face them all—alone?

She *had* to go back with a man of her own. He couldn't be just any man, either. She needed a husband with a passion to die for, who would make them all jealous with a lazy look her way or a possessive squeeze of her waist. It was all a fake, but she was desperate.

Surely someone in the precinct could fit the bill. But someone like that might walk away from the weekend with a few of her secrets under his belt. No, there wasn't anyone she could trust.

Jill swiveled sideways in her chair, her glance falling on her clipboard. She hadn't even been aware of what she'd written in the margin.... In bold scrawl there was the phone number from the radio ad. 1-800-HUSBAND.

Could she do it? It didn't take long to decide. Returning to Penny's wedding as a bride herself—even if it was for appearances only—was the best she could hope to do. With a shaking hand, she punched in the number....

* * * * *

Don't miss the next installment of the 1-800-HUSBAND miniseries! Watch for American Romance #601 THE LAST BRIDESMAID *by Leandra Logan—available October 1995!*

RUGGED. SEXY. HEROIC.

OUTLAWS and HEROES

Stony Carlton—A lone wolf determined never to be tied down.

Gabriel Taylor—Accused and found guilty by small-town gossip.

Clay Barker—At Revenge Unlimited, he *is* the law.

JOAN JOHNSTON, DALLAS SCHULZE and **MALLORY RUSH**, three of romance fiction's biggest names, have created three unforgettable men—modern heroes who have the courage to fight for what is right....

OUTLAWS AND HEROES—available in September wherever Harlequin books are sold.

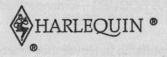 **HARLEQUIN** ®

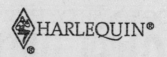

HARLEQUIN®

CHRISTMAS ROGUES

is giving you everything you want on your Christmas list this year:

- ✔ -great romance stories
- ✔ -award-winning authors
- ✔ -a FREE gift promotion
- ✔ -an abundance of Christmas cheer

This November, not only can you join ANITA MILLS, PATRICIA POTTER and MIRANDA JARRETT for exciting, heartwarming Christmas stories about roguish men and the women who tame them— but you can also receive a FREE gold-tone necklace or bracelet. (Details inside all copies of Christmas Rogues).

CHRISTMAS ROGUES—romance reading at its best—only from HARLEQUIN BOOKS!

Available in November wherever Harlequin books are sold.

HARLEQUIN®
AMERICAN ✦ ROMANCE®

IT'S A BABY BOOM!

NEW ARRIVALS

We're expecting—again! Join us for a reprisal of the New Arrivals promotion, in which special American Romance authors invite you to read about equally special heroines—all of whom are on a nine-month adventure! We expect each mom-to-be will find the man of her dreams—and a daddy in the bargain!

Watch for the newest arrival!

#600 ANGEL'S BABY
by Pamela Browning
September 1995

NA-3